Fina

"You boys don't want to do this," Clint said.

"Oh? Why not?" one asked.

"Because I didn't come here to kill anybody."

"In case you ain't noticed," one said, "we're two against you."

"Your guns look well used, but you fellas don't look like fast guns to me. And I don't even know how accurate you are. Looks to me like you're overmatched."

Suddenly, the two men were not so sure of themselves.

"Who the hell are you, anyway?" one finally asked.

"My name is Clint Adams, so making me draw my gun isn't really a good idea."

The two men stared at him.

"Adams?" one asked.

"The Gunsmith?" the other said.

"That's right," Clint said. "Now my best advice to you is to leave your guns where they are, in their holsters, and ride out. Now."

THE GUNSMITH

352

UNBOUND BY LAW

J. R. ROBERTS

JOVE BOOKS, NEW YORK

THE BERKLEY PUBLISHING GROUP
Published by the Penguin Group
Penguin Group (USA) Inc.
375 Hudson Street, New York, New York 10014, USA
Penguin Group (Canada), 90 Eglinton Avenue East, Suite 700, Toronto, Ontario M4P 2Y3, Canada
(a division of Pearson Penguin Canada Inc.)
Penguin Books Ltd., 80 Strand, London WC2R 0RL, England
Penguin Group Ireland, 25 St. Stephen's Green, Dublin 2, Ireland (a division of Penguin Books Ltd.)
Penguin Group (Australia), 250 Camberwell Road, Camberwell, Victoria 3124, Australia
(a division of Pearson Australia Group Pty Ltd.)
Penguin Books India Pvt. Ltd., 11 Community Centre, Panchsheel Park, New Delhi—110 017, India
Penguin Group (NZ), 67 Apollo Drive, Rosedale, North Shore 0632, New Zealand
(a division of Pearson New Zealand Ltd.)
Penguin Books (South Africa) (Pty.) Ltd., 24 Sturdee Avenue, Rosebank, Johannesburg 2196,
South Africa

Penguin Books Ltd., Registered Offices: 80 Strand, London WC2R 0RL, England

This is a work of fiction. Names, characters, places, and incidents either are the product of the author's imagination or are used fictitiously, and any resemblance to actual persons, living or dead, business establishments, events, or locales is entirely coincidental.

UNBOUND BY LAW

A Jove Book / published by arrangement with the author

PRINTING HISTORY
Jove edition / April 2011

Copyright © 2011 by Robert J. Randisi.
Cover illustration by Sergio Giovine.

ISBN: 978-0-515-14929-6

JOVE®
Jove Books are published by The Berkley Publishing Group,
a division of Penguin Group (USA) Inc.,
375 Hudson Street, New York, New York 10014.
JOVE® is a registered trademark of Penguin Group (USA) Inc.
The "J" design is a trademark of Penguin Group (USA) Inc.

PRINTED IN THE UNITED STATES OF AMERICA

10 9 8 7 6 5 4 3 2 1

ONE

The first tip-off was the buzzards.

"Easy, boy," Clint said, reining Eclipse in.

Ahead of them the sky was dotted with buzzards, circling. Not a lot, but enough to tell him that something bad had happened recently.

"Come on," he said, gigging the big Darley Arabian. "Somebody's in trouble and we're elected to help."

The sun was at its zenith in the New Mexico sky. The heat was not only coming down, but it was rising up from the baked ground.

Judging from the location of the flying scavengers, whatever had happened had taken place a couple of miles ahead. That the buzzards had not already closed in to feast could mean one of two things. First, ground scavengers had gotten there first. The birds were waiting for the coyotes to eat. Or, the people simply had not been dead long enough.

Or, second, there were survivors, and the buzzards were waiting for them to die.

Clint pushed Eclipse into a gallop, in case someone's survival depended on time.

The pair topped a rise and the carnage came into view. He reined in, looked down at the wagons. There were three of them, all upright, none burning. Around the wagons were bodies. Men, women, children, looked like about a dozen of them, apparently the remains of what had been three families.

He looked around, didn't see anyone else, then started down the hill slowly, carefully. When he reached the bottom, he approached the camp.

Okay, yeah, he could see a campfire, so the victims had been camped here. He dismounted, dropped Eclipse's reins to the ground, and approached the bodies on foot. Some were facedown, others faceup. Eleven bodies lying faceup had no apparent damage. They hadn't been stabbed, or shot. The other bodies he bent over, rolled them over just enough to see that they also had suffered no trauma. There were five children—three boys, two girls, between ages three to ten, he guessed.

The adults, what appeared to be three husbands and three wives. He matched them up as best he could, figuring the men and women lying close together would be couples. Two couples were in their late twenties, the other in their thirties, probably the parents of the oldest child, a girl.

Clint had a cold spot in the pit of his stomach as he studied the children.

The three wagons were covered. The contents seemed

to be each family's belongings—suitcases, tools, furniture.

He walked to the campfire, knelt by it, held his hand over the remains. Cold. There were plates and utensils in the dirt, the remnants of some meals that didn't look like breakfast. Apparently, whatever had happened to them had taken place after supper. Then, during the night, the fire had gone out. They hadn't even had time to get to their bedrolls.

He looked more closely at the ground. From the tracks there, he discerned coyotes had come into camp, maybe eaten some of the leftover food, but they hadn't been at the bodies yet.

Under normal circumstances, Clint would have buried the dead. But he felt that somebody had to examine these bodies, find out what had killed them. He decided to go to the nearest town and notify the law, maybe get a doctor out here to take a look at them.

There were a couple of towns, both due east. Carrizozo was the largest, Hondo the closest. If Hondo had a doctor, lawman, and telegraph, it made sense to go there. On the other hand, Carrizozo would certainly have all three.

He decided to go to the closest and hope he'd find all the help he needed there.

He took one last look around the camp, but couldn't find anything helpful. He looked up at the buzzards, wished he could bury the bodies to save them from being scavenged. In the end, he collected blankets from the bedrolls and wagons, covered each of the bodies, hoping that would do it. As he covered the body of a three-year-old girl his stomach flipped, and for a moment he thought he was going to lose his breakfast.

"Come on, big boy," he said, mounting Eclipse. "Let's go get some help."

A few miles away, he suddenly came upon the carcasses of a small band of coyotes. The bodies had already been visited upon by buzzards. He rode up to them, stared down. They had been worked over pretty good.

He dismounted, wrapped the smallest coyote up in his spare shirt, and tied it to his saddle—just in case by the time he returned, the carcasses were all gone.

He remounted and headed to Hondo.

TWO

He saw the telegraph lines before he reached town, so he was sure of that much.

Hondo was big enough to have what he wanted. He rode down the main street, saw the saloon, hotel, mercantile, finally the sheriff's office. No doctor's shingle, but that didn't mean anything. Maybe there was a doctor off the main street. At least there was an undertaker, right across from the sheriff.

He dismounted, looped Eclipse's reins over a post, and entered the sheriff's office.

It was small, dusty, but had all the trappings—potbellied stove, gun rack, cell block in the back. In one corner was a broom, but it didn't look as if it had been used very much.

The door to the office opened again and a man stepped in, wearing a badge and a scowl.

"Somebody said they saw somebody ride in," he said. "Sheriff Carl Scott."

"Clint Adams."

"The Gunsmith?" Scott asked. "What brings you to Hondo?"

"About fifteen miles from here, I came across three wagons. Looked like three families traveling together."

"So?"

"They're all dead."

"Dead?"

"Six adults, five kids."

"Indians? Comancheros?"

"They weren't attacked," Clint said. "There's not a mark on them."

"Then what killed them?"

"I don't know," Clint said. "It's going take a doctor to find that out."

The sheriff paused a moment, then asked, "Disease?"

"What disease kills with no marks? Open sores, something."

"I don't know."

"Like I said," Clint said. "It'll take a doctor. This town got one?"

"We do."

"We better go and talk to him, then, don't you think?"

"Sure, sure," Scott said. "I'll take you over there."

As they left the office, Clint noticed the sheriff's scowl had deepened.

The doctor's name was Doctor Eric Evans, according to his shingle. They entered the doctor's office, found the man setting a young boy's arm. The boy's mother stood alongside, wringing her hands.

"I'll be with you gents in a minute," Evans said in an accent Clint identified as German. He was a handsome man in his early forties.

They waited while he finished with the boy, who then walked out with his mother holding his good hand. "Maybe that's the last time you'll go climbing a tree," she scolded him.

As the door closed behind them, the doctor smiled at his visitors and said, "I doubt that will be the last time. He's broken that same arm three times. Now, what can I do for you gents?"

"Doc, this is Clint Adams. He found some dead bodies outside of town."

"Dead? How?" Evans asked Clint.

"I don't know," Clint said. "That's the problem."

"What do you mean? Seems to me a man with your reputation would be able to tell how some people were killed."

"Not these," Clint said. "Three families, five kids. All dead and not a mark on them."

"Curious."

"I also found some coyotes a few miles away from them, dead."

"Coyotes?"

"I brought one of them in with me."

"A dead coyote?" the sheriff asked. "What the hell for?"

"So somebody can figure out why it died," Clint said.

"Maybe the coyotes are carryin' some kind of disease that the families got?" the sheriff asked.

Clint looked at the doctor. "Wouldn't they have had

to be bitten?" he asked. "I didn't see any bites on any of them. And it'd have to be pretty odd for all of them to have been bitten, wouldn't it?"

"Yes, I think so," Evans said. "I shall have to ride out there to have a look. Will you show me?"

"Of course." Clint looked at the sheriff. "I think we should bring the undertaker, too."

"Yeah," the sheriff said. "I'll get 'im on our way out of town."

"I will saddle a horse," Evans said. "And bring my bag."

"What about the coyote I've got with me?" Clint asked.

"Bring it in," the doctor said. "I'll put it in the back and have a look at it when we get return. I think it's important to bring those people in."

"If there's anything left of them," the sheriff said.

"The buzzards were closing in," Clint admitted. "I covered the bodies with blankets."

"You should go and get yourself something to eat," the doctor said to Clint.

"And maybe a drink," Clint said. "One of those kids was only about three. A little girl."

"I'll meet you out front," the doctor said.

Clint left the office with the sheriff.

"Saloon's over there," Scott said. "Should be able to get a beer and some hardboiled eggs."

"That'll be enough for now," Clint said. "Say, Sheriff?"

"Yeah?"

"You didn't have three wagons of people here in town recently, did you?"

Scott scowled at Clint and said, "Don't you think I woulda told you that by now if we had?"

THREE

Out in front of the doctor's office a half an hour later, Clint was introduced to the undertaker, a man named E. B. Duff. He looked more like a banker than an undertaker: under six feet, wearing a brown suit and matching vest. He was seated aboard a buckboard when Clint got there. The doctor made the introduction.

"How many bodies you say we got out there?" he asked.

"Eleven," Clint said. "Six adults."

Duff looked back at his buckboard.

"I guess I can fit 'em. Jesus, what a damned shame. Children?"

"That's right," Clint said.

They turned as the sheriff came riding up.

"We ready to go?"

"Ready," Doctor Evans said.

"I'm ready, too," Clint said. He'd had a cold beer and a couple of hardboiled eggs, but he just felt thirstier and hungrier. He'd have to wait until they got back to have a full meal.

He mounted up.

"Lead the way, Mr. Adams," the sheriff said.

When they reached the campground, the four of them just sat where they were and surveyed the scene.

"My God," Duff said.

It looked to Clint like the bodies were still covered, the way he'd left them.

"We better get started loading the bodies onto E. B.'s buckboard."

"Go ahead," the doctor said, "but I want to examine a couple of them right away."

The doctor walked to one of the largest bodies, and then one of the smallest.

"Take these two last," he said.

"Like you say," the lawman agreed.

He and Duff walked to one of the blanket-covered bodies, looked down at it, then over to the doctor.

"Doc?" the sheriff called.

"Yes?" Evans had just uncovered the body of a man, and looked up at Sheriff Scott.

"You sure it's okay?"

The doctor knelt down next to the uncovered man, stared at him for a few moments. He turned the man's face one way, then the other, checked his hands and arms.

"I don't think this man died of any disease," he said. "Go ahead and load them, but keep them covered."

Scott and Duff eyed each other, then bent down and tucked in the edges of the blanket before lifting the first body and carrying it to the buckboard.

While the doctor continued to examine the dead man, Clint lifted one of the children's bodies and carried it to the buckboard.

They repeated the sequence until all but the two bodies Dr. Evans was examining were left—one man, and the little girl.

The three men watched as the soctor uncovered the little girl. He examined her closely, shaking his head.

"What do you see, Doc?" Clint asked.

"Just what you saw, Mr. Adams," he replied. "Nothing. No apparent damage."

"Then what killed them?" the sheriff asked.

"Or who?" Duff asked.

The doctor stood up. "Let's get these two on the buckboard, and when we get back to town I'll try to find out."

While Clint, the doctor, and E. B. Duff loaded the bodies onto the buckboard, the sheriff went into all three wagons, searching for something that would identify the families.

What bothered Clint was that the wagon tracks seemed to come from the direction of Hondo, yet the sheriff said the families had never stopped there.

"Doc?" he said while the sheriff was still inside one wagon.

"Yes, Mr. Adams?"

"Did you ever see any of these wagons in Hondo?"

The doctor frowned, looked around, then looked at Clint.

"I don't recall seeing these wagons or these people in town," he said. "Did you ask the sheriff the same question?"

"I did."

"What did he say?"

"Same thing you did."

"Then perhaps you should also ask Mr. Duff the same question," Evans said,

"No," Clint said, "that's okay. I guess I can believe the two of you."

The sheriff walked toward them carrying a collection of papers he had gathered from all three wagons.

"What've you got?" Duff asked.

"Letters, other papers," the sheriff said. "Might give me somebody to notify about these people. Or help me identify them."

Duff looked up at the buzzards, which were still circling.

"We better get these folks back to town," the undertaker said.

"Yeah, sure," the sheriff said.

He walked to his horse, stuffed the papers into his saddlebags.

"Got everything?" the doctor called.

"I think so." The sheriff mounted up.

"I don't think so," Clint said, but only the doctor heard him.

"What do you mean?"

"There's a question that hasn't been asked."

"And what's that?"

Clint waved his arm and asked, "What happened to these people's horses?"

FOUR

When they brought the bodies back to town, people lined up on either side of the street to watch. They rode first to the doctor's office, where they unloaded two of the bodies, and then to the undertaker's, where they then unloaded the remaining nine.

That done, Clint came together with the sheriff out front.

"What's next?" he asked.

"I'll let the undertaker do his job, the doctor do his. I'll go to my office, look through these papers and try to do my job."

"I'm going to get a hotel room, a bath, and a meal," Clint said. "You mind if I check in with you to see what you've found out?"

"Sure, why not?"

"Thanks," Clint said. "I'd like to find out who these poor people were."

"I understand," Sheriff Scott said. "After all, you're the

one who found them. If I was you, I'd get a room at the Heritage Hotel. Best in town."

"Thanks for the advice. I'm taking my horse to the livery. You?"

"I got someplace else to take him," Scott said. "See you later."

They walked their horses in separate directions.

Clint got Eclipse taken care of, registered in the Heritage Hotel, then got himself a bath. He was ready for a meal afterward, but first he went over to the doctor's office.

"Come on in," Evans said as Clint stuck his head in the man's office.

"The bodies?"

"In the other room." The doctor sat down at his desk and turned to rifle through some papers.

"Did you find out what killed them?"

"Not exactly."

"What's that mean?"

Evans swiveled his chair around to face Clint.

"They didn't have a disease, and they did not die by violence."

"What else does that leave?"

The doctor studied Clint for a moment, then said, "I believe those people were poisoned."

FIVE

"Poisoned?"

Evans nodded.

"But . . . how? Why?"

"I can't answer those questions," Doc Evans said. "In fact, I can't be sure I'm right."

"How can you *be* sure?"

"I'll have to send some blood samples to the state capital to have them tested," the doctor said.

"That'll take some time."

"Indeed, it will."

"These people need to be buried."

"And they will be," Evans said. "I'll take samples from all of them, first. Then I'll pack them in ice, and ship some of them to the state capital. Once they arrive, my reply can come by telegraph."

"Santa Fe's days away," Clint said.

"If I can get the samples on a stage this week, we could have a reply by the end of next week."

Clint frowned. Did he want to stay in Hondo that long, waiting to hear how these strangers had died?

"Well," Clint said, "let me know what I can do. I'm going to go and get something to eat. Interested?"

"I think I'd better get to work collecting samples," Doctor Evans said. "If you go to the café right around the corner, I'll join you . . . if you're still there when I finish."

"Around the corner," Clint said. "I'll try it. Thanks."

He left the doctor's office and walked around the corner to the suggested café. As he entered and breathed in the smells, he knew the man had steered him in the right direction.

A waiter showed him to a table away from the front windows. He ordered a steak dinner and coffee.

The sheriff looked up as his office door slammed open and Mayor Tolbert entered.

Fred Tolbert had been mayor for many years. Once totally absorbed with his civic duty, his resolve had waned over the years; these days, he was mostly concerned with what was right for Mayor Fred Tolbert.

"What the hell is goin' on, Sheriff?" he demanded. The words came out encased in a cloud of cigar smoke.

"Whaddaya mean, Mayor?"

"I heard you brought in three families who died of some kind of plague. Are you crazy?"

"I don't know where you heard that, Mayor, but it's bad information."

"You didn't bring them in?"

"We did bring them in, but they didn't die of any plague."

"How can you be sure?"

"The doctor examined the bodies on the spot, said they wasn't sick."

"How can he be sure?"

"Well, that you're gonna have to ask him, Mayor," the lawman said.

The mayor filled the small office with his bulk. At sixty-five, he was the heaviest he'd ever been, and it seemed he was continuing to expand.

"I knew we never should've let that German bastard set up shop here," he muttered.

"Town needed a doctor, Mayor."

"Yeah, it did," the mayor said. "Yeah, okay, I'll have to go and talk to him."

"If I was you, I'd keep that stuff about him bein' a German bastard to myself," Scott advised.

The mayor ignored the comment. "Who found the bodies?"

"A fella who just happened to be passin' by."

"So? Who was it?"

"Clint Adams."

"Wha— You mean, the Gunsmith?"

"That's right."

"What the hell—is he in town now?"

"He is."

"Well, that's not good," the mayor said. "We don't need that kind of trouble."

"So far all he's done is find three families who'd somehow been killed and report it. Then he went back out there to help us bring the bodies in. Can't say he caused all that much trouble."

"Why didn't he go to Carrizozo and report it?" the mayor demanded.

"We're closer."

"They're bigger."

"Too late, Mayor," Scott said. "What's done is done, you know?"

"And what's the doctor doin?"

"Far as I know, he's tryin' to find out what killed them."

"They weren't shot?"

"They weren't shot, stabbed, clubbed, or anythin' else violent."

"Sounds like the plague to me."

"You start spreadin' that word around, Mayor, and there will be trouble."

"I ain't gonna spread it around, Carl," the mayor responded. "Damn it, I ain't an idiot!"

Sheriff Scott didn't comment on that.

"Where's Adams now?" Tolbert demanded.

"Probably in the hotel."

"Which one?"

"The Heritage."

The mayor frowned. He owned the Guest House Hotel, the only other hotel in town.

"Why did he choose that one?"

Scott shrugged.

"Well, damn it, I guess I'll have to talk to the doctor."

"I think so," Scott said.

The mayor wagged a thick index finger at the lawman. "If this turns out to be some kind of disease—"

"I know," the sheriff said, "it'll mean my badge."

The mayor huffed out.

SIX

The mayor did not find the doctor in his office. Rather, he found him at the undertaker's, taking blood samples from the dead bodies.

"What the hell are you doin'?" he demanded when he found Evans leaning over one of the dead children.

"I need to take blood samples and send them to Santa Fe," the doctor said.

"What the hell for?"

"To prove my poison theory."

"You think these people were poisoned? You sure they didn't die of some disease?"

"I do, and no, they did not die of a disease."

"By who?"

Evans straightened and looked at the mayor.

"I have no way of knowing that, Mayor," he said. "That will be up to the law to discover."

"The law? Not our sheriff. Why should he spend his time on that?"

"He's the one who brought them in."

"If you're sending samples to the capital, then ask them to send their own investigators here to find out who poisoned those people."

"That's not my job, Mayor," Evans said. "It's yours. Now, if you'll leave me to it, I'll finish what *is* my job."

He turned his back on the mayor and went back to his task.

On his way out, the mayor stopped and wagged his big finger at E. B. Duff.

"You get these people in the ground as soon as you can, E. B. You understand?"

"Sure, Mayor," Duff said. "After all, that's my job, right?"

"Just get it done," Tolbert said. "This ain't good for this town. You should have checked with me before you went out and picked up those bodies."

"Sheriff said I should do it, Mayor," Duff said with a shrug. "And he's the sheriff."

"Never mind!" the mayor said. "Right now just do what *I* tell you!"

Duff had no chance to reply as the mayor went storming out the door.

Clint enjoyed his steak dinner at the small café, and had a second pot of coffee to wash down a good piece of peach pie.

He was just finishing up, having given up on the doctor, when the man walked in the door. He quickly spotted Clint and came over.

"I ate as slow as I could," Clint said.

Evans sat across from Clint.

"Well, it takes time to take blood from eleven bodies, and the mayor slowed me down."

"The mayor? What did he have to do with it?"

The waiter came over and Evans ordered a piece of pie. He poured himself a cup of coffee from Clint's second pot while he waited.

"He came in like he usually does, all bluster and demanded to know what I was doing."

"He's not happy we brought those bodies in, huh?"

"Not at all. I just hope he doesn't start talking about disease," the doctor said. "He could start a panic."

"Isn't he responsible enough to know that?"

"He might have been, once," Evans said. "I came here a few years ago. I am not impressed with him."

"How long has he been mayor?"

"A long time," Evans said. "Too long."

The waiter came with Evan's apple pie and set it in front of him.

"That's all you're going to eat?"

"I've got to get those blood samples on ice before the heat gets to them," he said.

"Where are you going to get the ice?"

"The owner of one of the saloons owes me a favor," he said. "He has an icehouse behind the saloon with kegs of beer in it."

"I hope he doesn't mind putting blood in there with his beer."

"I'll assure him it's safe."

"If the mayor came to see you he must have seen the sheriff already."

"I'd assume so."

"Which means he knows about me."

"I didn't say anything."

"No, but the sheriff would have to," Clint said.

"Well, then, you'll be talking to the mayor as well," Evans said. "You can form your own opinion."

"Guess I better go and talk to the mayor," Clint said. "Right after I have another cup of coffee."

SEVEN

Clint found the sheriff sitting at his desk.

"No deputies?" he asked as he entered.

"Town's too cheap to pay for 'em," Scott said. "Have a seat."

Clint sat in a wooden chair across from the sheriff.

"Heard your mayor's been going around town complaining."

"Yeah, I guess he thinks I shoulda just left eleven people lying out there to rot."

"What's your next move?"

"Somethin' I shoulda done today," the lawman said. "In the mornin', I'm goin' back out there to see if I can figure out what happened to their horses. And where they came from."

"Mind if I tag along?"

"Don't mind at all," the lawman said. "You noticed those wagon tracks looked like they were comin' from this direction?"

"I noticed."

"They weren't here, Adams," he said. "Ask anybody."

"I did. I asked the doctor. He backed you."

"What's the doc doin'?"

"Getting some blood ready to send to Santa Fe to be checked," Clint said.

"What for?"

The doctor had given Clint the okay to talk to the sheriff about poison.

"He thinks they were poisoned, but he needs somebody to examine the blood to be sure."

"Poisoned? Who the hell would poison three families? Including children?"

"Beats me," Clint said. "Must have been something personal, though."

"Those coyotes did die," Scott said. "And they must've eaten some of the food that was left on the fire."

"Once the fire went out."

"What's the doc doin' with that coyote you brought in?"

"You know, I didn't ask. But I assume the coyote's blood will also be going to the capital."

"The mayor stopped back in here again after he spoke to the doctor and the undertaker."

"What did he have to say then?"

"Doesn't want me investigatin'," Scott said. "He says it's not my job."

"Whose job does he think it is?"

"The state," Scott said. "He thinks a federal marshal should come in and have a look, and that I should stay out of it."

"What do you think about that?" Clint asked.

"I think I kinda felt the same way he does when you first came to me," the lawman admitted. "But since I've seen the bodies of those kids, I'd like to find out what sonofabitch killed them."

"So would I."

"Well, we can head out early in the mornin'," Scott said. "You can meet me out front about eight."

Clint stood up. "I'll be here."

"You any good at trackin'?" the lawman asked.

"Pretty good."

"Good," Scott said, "because I ain't worth shit when it comes to readin' signs."

EIGHT

Clint met up with the sheriff in front of his office early the next morning. He'd had a quick breakfast in the Heritage Hotel's dining room.

The night before, he'd had a few beers at one of the saloons in town. He wondered at the time if it was the same saloon the doctor had been talking about. Then he decided, since he was drinking beer, not to think about it.

He went to his room early, tired from the day. After an hour of reading he turned in, and woke when the sun came through his window.

Now, after saddling Eclipse, he had walked the horse over to the sheriff's office, where the lawman was waiting by his horse. He held up a burlap sack as Clint got closer.

"I brought just a few supplies, in case we're away longer than expected."

"Good. Shall we go?"

They mounted up and rode out to the campsite.

* * *

As they rode along Clint asked, "Did you find out anything from the papers you took from the wagons?"

"Some names," Scott said. "I came up with one last
name—Anderson. I don't know if all three families had
that same name."

"Could be the women married men with different
names," Clint said. "There could be brothers and sisters,
or all brothers."

"I've sent a telegram to the authorities in Baltimore.
That was the return address on some of the letters. Looks
like the family's name was Eckert."

"Anything else?"

"Some children's names," the lawman said. "Johnny,
Beth, Megan . . . don't know which kids, but at least that's
something."

"Maybe, by the time we're done, we'll have all their
names for headstones," Clint said.

"That's what I'm hoping."

"You surprise me, Sheriff."

"How so, Adams?"

"When I first met you, you didn't seem too thrilled
about me being here," Clint explained. "Or about coming out here with me."

"When we met," Scott admitted, "I had a helluva hang-
over. Sorry."

"Problems?"

"At home," Scott said.

"Wife?"

Scott nodded. "Maybe not for much longer, though,"
he said. "She's not happy here, wants me to quit my job
and leave town."

"And you don't want to?"

"I don't know," the lawman said. "I'm not as sure of things as she is."

"How long have you been married?" Clint asked.

"Ten years. You?"

"Never been."

"Do you have a home?"

"My saddle, mostly," Clint said. "I'm not the type to put down roots."

"Never came close?" the sheriff asked.

"Once," Clint said, "but she died."

"Too bad. I'm sorry."

"It was a long time ago."

They passed the place where the dead coyotes had been. They were all but gone—just some bones left behind by the buzzards.

When they reached the wagons, all was as it had been when they left. There was nothing left for the scavengers to be interested in—and, apparently, no two-legged scavengers had come along.

The men dismounted.

"I'm gonna go through the wagons again, see if I missed anythin'," Scott said.

"I'm going to walk around, see what kind of signs, if any, I can find."

Scott nodded, walked to one of the wagons, and climbed in.

Clint could hear the sheriff going through the wagons while he walked the camp, studying the ground. He found it odd that the only hoof prints he could find had apparently come from the wagon teams. It looked as if no one had ridden into camp, or out, on a saddle mount.

"Anythin'?" Scott called.

"I can't find any sign of anyone else in camp," Clint said. "Just the families."

"I found some weapons," Scott said. "Rifles, hand-guns. They kept them in the wagons."

"Very trusting of them. Didn't find any on the bodies, right?"

"No."

Clint waved at the ground. "This concerns me."

"Why?"

"All signs indicate there was no one else in camp with these families."

"So?"

"It means if they were poisoned, they were poisoned somewhere else," Clint said. "Or, their food was poisoned somewhere else."

"So they ate once and died," the sheriff said. "That means if the food was poisoned, it happened a day's ride from here. Somewhere they stopped."

"Unless it was a slow-acting poison," Clint said. "Maybe they had to ingest it more than once."

"But the coyotes seem to have died from it," the lawman pointed out.

"They did, but they're smaller animals," Clint said. "Anyway, I don't know that much about poison. We should leave that to the doctor, I guess."

"Agreed."

"Maybe," Clint said, "we should load everything of value onto one wagon, go back to town, get a team, and drive it back. Eventually, somebody's going to come along and help themselves."

"True," the sheriff said. "We could save the stuff for the family back East."

"If there is any."

"But we came out here to find out somethin'," Scott said.

"Yes, we did. So before we do that, I guess we better backtrack on these wagon tracks and see where they were coming from."

"They head off toward Hondo," Scott said, "but they must turn off somewhere."

"Then let's mount up and find out."

NINE

They followed the wagon tracks back toward Hondo and, as they suspected, they turned off halfway back, heading east.

Or, more to the point, they had come from the east.

"What's that way?" Clint asked.

"Several small towns," the sheriff said. "Geneva, Canyon, Coldwater . . ."

"How small?"

"Smaller than Hondo."

"Could they have outfitted in one of them?"

"Sure," Scott said. "There's a mercantile or trading post, in all of them. They'd be able to get some supplies."

"And food."

"Yeah, and food."

"If we follow these tracks," Clint said, "will it take you out of your jurisdiction?"

"I'm already out," Scott said. "I'm just a town sheriff, you know."

"Well," Clint said, "I could go, and you could return to town, come back with a team, and take one of the wagons back with you."

"And what will you do?"

"Check out those towns, see which one they came from," Clint said.

"Clint," Scott said, "we still don't know for sure that they were poisoned. It's still a theory from the doctor."

"I know it," Clint said, "but I could ask some questions. It'd be better than just sitting around in the hotel, or the saloon."

"I could go with you . . ."

"Yeah, you could," Clint said, "but then you'd have to be away from town overnight. That would leave Hondo without a lawman."

"So?" Sheriff Scott asked. "The drunks will have to put themselves to bed in a cell, for a change."

"No," Clint said, "I'll go alone, see what I can find out, and then come back. You go back to town, be the sheriff. You don't want to upset your mayor."

Scott opened his mouth, as if to say something, but caught himself. Instead, he said, "Okay. Here." He handed over the burlaps sack. "Just some coffee, beef jerky—and a bottle of whiskey."

"Whiskey?"

"For snakebites," Scott said.

"The kind that leave hangovers behind?"

"Yeah," Scott said, "that kind."

"Tell me in what order I'll come to these towns," Clint said.

"Coldwater first, then Geneva, then Canyon."

"And after that?"

"If you go farther than that," Scott said, "it means you've gone too far. It'll take you a while to get back."

Clint tied the sack to his saddle, then extended his hand to the lawman, who shook it. "I'll see you in a few days."

"Don't take any chances," Scott said. "Each of those towns has a lawman. Check in with them."

"I usually do. Do they have telegraph offices?"

"No, they're too small for that."

"Okay," Clint said, "I'll just introduce myself, and hope they believe me."

"They will."

"How do you know?"

"You have a sincere face—and you're the Gunsmith."

TEN

"Where've you been?"

Johnny Devlin stared at his boss a bit sheepishly.

"I had to camp overnight," Devlin said.

"And?" Harry Cantrell asked.

"I, uh, overslept."

Cantrell was undoubtedly the most successful businessman in the town of Roswell. He also had many businesses in the larger town of Carrizozo, but had not yet become as successful there.

"You're the only man I know who can sleep on the ground and oversleep," he said to his man.

"Sorry, boss."

"How did it go?"

"Just like you planned."

"Did you stay around to see if anyone found them?" Cantrell asked.

"Uh, no, you didn't tell me to do that."

"Oh, I forgot," Cantrell said. "You only do exactly what you're told to do."

Devlin frowned, wondering what else he was supposed to do. He always did what he was told.

"Okay, Johnny," Cantrell said. "Go get yourself a drink."

"Sure, boss."

"I'm leaving for Carrizozo today. I won't be back here for a couple of weeks."

"Uh, am I gonna get paid before you go?"

"Oh, sure." Cantrell opened his top drawer, took out some money, and held it out to Devlin.

"Thanks, boss."

"You need anything else while I'm gone, talk to Grant."

Grant Sutcliffe was Cantrell's "partner" in Roswell. He thought he was a full partner, but there was a lot going on behind the scenes that Sutcliffe didn't know about, and never would. Even Cantrell's partner in Carrizozo didn't know everything that was going on. Harry Cantrell was not full partners with anyone but himself.

"Okay, boss."

"Or send me a telegram."

"Right."

"You know how to send a telegram, don't you?"

Devlin looked hurt. "Sure, boss."

"Okay, then get out," Cantrell said. "Have a couple of beers."

"If you say so, boss," Devlin said, and left.

Once Devlin was gone, Cantrell packed his saddlebags, mostly with money that he would deposit into his bank account when he got back to Carrizozo. His trips to Roswell were usually only to collect his profits. This time there had been trouble that he'd had to take care of, and only Johnny Devlin knew the details of that. Actually, Devlin was reliable because the man did everything he was told. It didn't matter much that he had no initiative. In fact, it was preferable. He didn't need somebody like Devlin all of a sudden thinking he had brains.

Sutcliffe was a different story. He was a good businessman, but there was no reason for him to know what was going on behind the scenes. Cantrell preferred not to have to explain his decisions to anyone. The days when he had to justify himself to others were long gone.

Harry Cantrell was well on his way to being the biggest businessman in all of New Mexico, and he wasn't about to explain his methods to anyone.

Johnny Devlin did have the ability to make up his own mind when came to his vices. His boss had told him to go and have a couple of beers, but when he entered the Red Sand Saloon and went to the bar he said, "Whiskey."

He knew men who said beer cut trail dust better than anything, but for Devlin it was whiskey. And after a few glasses of whiskey, his other vice popped up—literally. Drinking whiskey always got Johnny Devlin in the mood for a whore.

"Thanks, Barney," he said, and left.

Even Barney the bartender knew where Devlin headed after a few drinks.

By the time the whore got down on her knees in front of Devlin, he was ready to pop. She undid the buttons on his trousers and reached in, drawing out his impressive erection.

Her name was Goldy, and the first time she'd ever seen Johnny Devlin naked she'd been impressed, thought she was in for some kind of ride. However, as she began to work on that big, hard cock it suddenly went off, splashing her face and chest copiously.

And the same thing happened again, this time. She had barely began to stroke Devlin when he groaned and sprayed.

Too bad such a big, lovely, hard cock exploded if a whore just looked at it.

ELEVEN

Clint followed the wagon tracks for several hours before they veered off again. Apparently they had not come from any of the three towns Sheriff Scott mentioned. Now the tracks were coming from the southeast, and Clint wasn't sure what was ahead of him. He was now heading south, which was where Hondo was, but he was also heading east, which was taking him farther from that town.

It was also taking him over much tougher terrain. The ground was baked so hard that it yielded no tracks. All he could do was keep traveling in that general direction and hope he'd happen upon the trail once again.

He came upon a collection of small buildings that could barely be called a town, decided to stop and see what—if anything—they could tell him.

There was a trading post that looked to be the only business that was open, with a couple of horses tied off in front of it.

He looped Eclipse's reins carelessly around the post

and went inside. He could have let the reins hang loosely, secure in the knowledge that the Darley Arabian would never wander off, but that might tempt someone to try to walk away with the horse.

When he entered, he saw that the place was not just a trading post, but had a bar and even offered haircuts and baths.

"Welcome, stranger!" the man behind the bar greeted. He was a portly, middle-aged man with a completely bald head. "Lookin' to purchase some supplies, or cut the dust with a drink? Or both?"

"I think I'll start with a drink, for now."

"Beer or whiskey?"

Clint looked at the two men who were standing at the bar. One had a beer, and the other had whiskey.

"What do you boys suggest?" he asked.

The two men, who looked as if they'd been riding hard, both turned to look at him.

"Beer's warm," one of them said.

"Whiskey's watered down," the other said.

"Hey, hey . . ." the proprietor said.

"I'll have the beer," Clint said. "At least it'll be wet."

"It ain't all that bad," the barman said, obviously hurt by the comments.

A flat-looking beer was set in front of Clint. He took one sip and saw what the two men had meant.

"A nickel," the barman said.

"Robbery," one of the men said.

Clint dropped a nickel on the bar and took another sip of the beer he knew he'd drink no more of.

"I'm looking for some information," he said to the barman.

"Oh? What kind of information?"

"I'm trying to find out if three families in three wagons may have gone by here in the past few days."

"Three wagons?" the barman repeated.

"Loaded with belongings," Clint said. "Six adults traveling with five children."

"What'd they do?" the beer drinker asked.

Clint looked at the two men, who were staring at him with interest.

"They didn't do anything," Clint said. "They had it done to them. They're all dead."

"Dead?" the proprietor said, again offering no information, simply repeating.

"Even the kids?" the whiskey drinker asked.

"Yes," Clint said, "even the kids."

"That ain't right," the beer drinker said.

"No," Clint said, "it's not."

"You law?" the whiskey drinker asked.

Clint decided to tell the truth. There didn't seem to be any harm in it.

"No, I'm not," he said. "But I'm the one who found them on the trail. All dead, all with no marks on them."

"No marks?"

Clint was getting tired of the bartender.

"So what killed 'em?" the beer drinker asked.

"Don't know," Clint said. "The doctors are checking that out now. I'm just trying to find out where they came from."

"And you ain't wearin' tin?" the whiskey drinker asked.

"No," Clint said. "This is just something I want to do. I want to find out what—or who—killed them."

He looked at the bartender. "Did they come through

here? I lost their tracks south of here, but it looks like they were coming from this direction."

"I ain't seen 'em," the barman said. "I'd remember three wagonloads of folks."

"How about you boys?" Clint asked. "Seen anything? Wagons? Maybe some sign?"

They both shook their heads.

"We ain't seen nothin'," the beer drinker said.

"Wish we could help," the whiskey drinker said.

"Where'd you find 'em?" Beer Drinker asked.

"Just outside of Hondo."

"Hondo," Whiskey Drinker said. "That's southwest of here, ain't it?"

"That's right."

"Where are them folks now?" Whiskey asked.

"We took them into Hondo for the doctor and undertaker to care for."

"And the wagons?" Beer asked.

"Still out there."

The two men looked at each other, and Clint had a sudden suspicion they weren't asking their questions simply out of curiosity.

"The Hondo sheriff was going to take them in, though," he added. "He's probably done it by now. At least, he was going to take in all their valuables."

Again, the two men exchanged a look.

"You sayin' we was thinkin' about stealin' somethin'?" Beer Drinker asked.

"I don't think I said that."

"Sounds like that's what you was thinkin'," Whiskey Drinker said.

"Look," Clint said, "you can take it any way you want. I was just giving you the story."

Both men turned to face him, hard looks on their faces, well-used guns on their hips.

TWELVE

"Now take it easy, boys."

"You ain't no law," Beer said.

"And you insulted us," Whiskey said.

Clint looked at the barman.

"I dint hear nuthin'," he said, raising his hands.

"Look," Clint said to the two men, "I've got to get moving. Just finish your drinks and calm down."

He turned and went out the door. He was reaching for Eclipse's reins when he heard them come out onto the boardwalk behind him.

"Not so fast!" one of them said.

Now that they didn't have drinks in front of them he couldn't tell them apart.

"Not so fast."

It didn't matter which repeated the phrase. This was just getting stupid.

"You boys don't want to do this," Clint said.

"Oh? Why not?" one asked.

"Because I didn't come here to kill anybody."

"In case you ain't noticed," one said, "we're two against you."

"Your guns look well used, but you fellas don't look like fast guns to me. And I don't even know how accurate you are. Looks to me like you're overmatched."

Suddenly, the two men were not so sure of themselves.

"Who the hell are you, anyway?" one finally asked.

"If I tell you that," Clint said, "you'll just think I'm showing off."

Now the two men exchanged a glance, wondering what they'd stepped into.

"If you're so good with a gun," one of them said, "show us somethin'."

"I don't show off with my gun," Clint said. "If you want to see something, you'll have to go for your guns."

Now they flexed their hands and fingers nervously.

"Okay, here it is," Clint said. "I figure you boys were thinking of salvaging some stuff from those wagons I told you about. The sheriff of Hondo really is collecting the valuables to send to the families back East. So that's a bad idea."

The two men nodded, listening intently.

"And my name is Clint Adams," he went on, "so making me draw my gun really isn't a good idea."

The two men stared at him.

"Adams?" one asked.

"The Gunsmith?" the other asked.

"That's right," Clint said. "Now, my best advice to you is to leave your guns where they are, in their holsters, and ride out. Now."

He didn't have to tell the two of them twice. They

both hurried to their horses, mounted up, and rode off.

"You really the Gunsmith?" the proprietor asked from the doorway.

"I am," Clint said.

"Hell," the man said. "The Gunsmith in my place."

"Yeah, see how many more customers that gets you," Clint suggested.

Clint grabbed Eclipse's reins and mounted up, then turned to face the proprietor.

"You sure you didn't see any sign of those wagons?" he asked.

"Mister," the man said, "if three wagonloads of people pulled up here, don't you think I'd remember it?"

"I suppose you would," Clint said. "But if they stopped here to eat and then died of poisoning on the trail, you wouldn't want to admit that, would you?"

"Wha-what?" The guy looked at Clint, his eyes popping. "What's that you say?"

Clint felt the man's reaction was genuine.

"Never mind," Clint said. "Thanks for the beer."

He turned Eclipse and continued to ride southeast.

THIRTEEN

Clint camped without finding the tracks again.

Glad that the sheriff had given him the meager sack of supplies, he made himself some coffee and supped on dried beef jerky.

He had passed a signpost earlier that told him Roswell was twenty miles ahead. For want of a better idea, he figured when he woke in the morning, he'd just head for Roswell and see what he could find there. Maybe even send Sheriff Scott a telegram.

He didn't see any reason not to turn in. He doubted the two men from the trading post would come looking for him in the dark. Even if they did, Eclipse would alert him if anyone neared the camp.

In any case, he removed his gun belt, folded it over, and set it right by his head. That done, he allowed himself to drift off to sleep.

* * *

When Clint woke the next morning, he had a cup of coffee that was left in the pot, doused the fire, stowed the coffeepot, and saddled Eclipse.

They headed for Roswell.

The wagon tracks reappeared a few miles from Roswell. They came from the town, then veered off, which explained why he hadn't seen them for a while.

He wondered why the tracks kept veering off every so often, wondered still if the poison had already been working on the families? Maybe they had been disoriented?

The horses, left to their own devices, probably would have continued to go straight.

Back at the campsite, Clint had studied the ground, wondering how the wagon teams could have gotten free. If someone had released them, he'd managed to hide his tracks from Clint who—while not an expert—was a pretty good reader of signs. Maybe someone mounted had let them free, their horse's tracks hidden by those left behind by the teams. Had to be six horses, and anyone who knew what he was doing could have camouflaged his own tracks.

Clint wondered if there might have been someone else among the family members who had done the poisoning, and then released the horses.

Who would the family have allowed to ride with them? Or might they have picked a stranger up along the way?

What kind of a man would sit with those eleven people—including five children—poison them, and watch them die?

Maybe the answers were in Roswell.

*   *   *

Roswell was a much larger town than Hondo. The main street was a busy thoroughfare and hardly anyone paid attention to Clint as he rode in. That suited him. He had to pause twice to let wagons go by, but spotted both the sheriff's office and a large saloon before he finally came to the livery stable.

As he was putting Eclipse in the hands of the liveryman, Clint was trying to decide what his course of action should be. He had no reason to trust anyone in Roswell. If this was where those families were poisoned, it could have been anyone. Did he really want to announce his presence to the local sheriff?

He decided to check into a hotel, then walk over to the sheriff's office and introduce himself. He wouldn't tell him why he was there, just take his measure. After that, he intended to send a telegram to Hondo and see what Sheriff Scott knew about Roswell's lawman.

He hefted his saddlebags over his shoulder, grabbed his rifle, and walked to the closest hotel. He only intended to stay one night, so the quality of the hotel was of little consequence.

Once he was registered and had deposited his bags in the room, he crossed the street and walked along to the sheriff's office. The Roswell sheriff was much better situated than Sheriff Scott: The office was new, three times the size, kept clean, with a modern stove against the wall and a cellblock that was on a second floor.

"Nice place," he said to the man behind the desk. He was in his forties, clean-shaven with a recent haircut, pleasant looking, but fit.

"Roswell's growing, and we're growing with it," the

sheriff said. "Of course, if they bring in a modern police force, I'll be out. But why am I telling you this? Sheriff Dean Turner. What can I do for you, sir?"

"My name's Clint Adams, Sheriff," he said. "I just wanted to check in with you. I just rode into town."

"I see," Turner said. "What's the Gunsmith's business is Roswell?"

"No business," Clint said. "I'm just riding through. I like to check in with the local law whenever I ride into a town."

"Sounds like a good idea," the sheriff said. "How long will you be staying?"

"A day, maybe two," Clint said. "Certainly no more."

Maybe long enough, Clint thought, to come up with a good story about why he'd be interested in three families traveling by wagon.

"Where are you staying?"

"Hotel closest to the livery," Clint said. "It was convenient."

"It's an okay place," the lawman said. "Well, as long as you avoid trouble, I don't have any problem with you being in Roswell, Mr. Adams."

"Thanks, Sheriff," Clint said. "You'd be surprised how many lawmen try to come up with a reason to run me out of town in the first hour."

"If I need to do that, I've got a couple of deputies I can rely on. Keep that in mind, and we'll get along fine."

"Suits me," Clint said. "Thanks very much, Sheriff. Maybe I can buy you a drink while I'm in town."

"That suits me," the sheriff said. "Maybe I'll see you later."

"Have a good day, Sheriff."

Clint left the office, feeling satisfied—for the moment.

FOURTEEN

The wagon tracks had led him into Roswell, but once he'd reached the main street they had disappeared among all the other tracks that crisscrossed the street.

He found the telegraph office without asking anyone where it was. He didn't want anyone remembering him for asking.

He entered the telegraph office and had time to compose his message while the clerk took care of another customer ahead of him.

The clerk sent it while he waited.

TO SHERIFF SCOTT, HONDO, N.M.
AM IN ROSWELL. APPRECIATE ANY HELPFUL INFORMATION.
CLINT ADAMS

He hoped Sheriff Scott would read between the lines and tell him what he needed to know.

"Will you wait for a reply, sir?"

"Yes," Clint said. "I'll sit outside."

"I'll bring it right out as soon as it comes."

Clint expected Scott to be in his office, or certainly in town, so a reply should come fairly quickly.

He grabbed a straight backed wooden chair from inside, carried it out with him and got comfortable.

Sheriff Turner entered the office of Grant Sutcliffe, startling the man behind his desk.

"Didn't hear you knock, Sheriff."

"That's because I didn't. Where's Cantrell?"

"Left town, went back to Carrizozo yesterday. What's wrong?"

"Nothin'," the Sheriff said. "I forgot, that's all. Where'd Devlin go?"

"If I know him, probably in a saloon or a whorehouse," Sutcliffe said.

"Yeah, you're probably right. Okay, I'll find him."

"Is it something I can help with, Sheriff?" Sutcliffe asked.

Sheriff Turner stared at Harry Cantrell's partner. Sutcliffe was about ten years younger than Cantrell and had a good head for business, but didn't know half of what Cantrell was into.

Turner reported to Cantrell, not Sutcliffe.

"No, Mr. Sutcliffe," Turner said. "Sorry I bothered you."

Goldy was surprised.

She'd been sucking Johnny Devlin's pretty cock for almost a minute before he exploded. Maybe the drunker she got him, the longer he'd last. If only he'd last long enough for her to get that cock inside of her.

Devlin moaned, rolled over onto his side, and started to snore almost immediately.

She got off the bed, pulled on her robe. She'd managed to avoid the spray this time, the advantage of having Devlin on his back. He'd messed up his own belly and chest, and then rolled over onto it.

She left the room and went downstairs to tell the madam she'd need another room if she was going to keep working. When she got there, the sheriff was talking to the madam, whose name was Rose.

"Goldy," Rose said, "is Devlin upstairs?"

"Yeah, passed out," she said. "The room's gonna need cleaning, Rose, and I'll need another one."

Rose looked at the sheriff.

"You wanna go up and get him?"

"No," Turner said, "but I do have to talk to him. I'll have someone come and get him, one of my deputies."

As he went out the door, Rose said, "Goldy, take room six . . ."

FIFTEEN

"Here's your answer, Mr. Adams," the clerk said, reaching his arm out the door.

"Thanks."

Clint took the telegram and unfolded it. It was from Sheriff Scott.

WATCH YOUR STEP.

That was Scott's way of warning him to watch out for everyone in Roswell, even Sheriff Turner. At least, that's the way he took it.

He folded the telegram, stood up, and stuck the note in his pocket. He was going to have to ask his questions while steering away from Sheriff Turner. That meant mostly bartenders. But before he started hitting saloons, he went back to the livery stable.

"Not takin' that horse outta here already, are ya?" the liveryman asked.

"No," Clint said. "He needs some rest."

"That's some animal, I gotta tell ya," the old man said. "In all my years, I ain't never seen a finer one."

"Thanks. What's your name, old-timer?"

"Name's Jim Hacker. I prefer Jim to 'old-timer,'" he said.

"Sorry," Clint said, "I didn't mean offense."

"That's okay. If ya ain't takin' yer horse out, why'd ya come back?"

"I need to ask somebody some questions," Clint said. "You look like a man who knows what's going on in town."

"I keep my ears open," Hacker admitted. "First, who are ya?"

"My name's Clint Adams."

"Ya don't say!" Hacker replied gleefully. "The Gunsmith, in my place? Figures you'd have a horse like that. Well, what kin I do for ya?"

"I'm looking for any sign of three wagons that might have passed through here in the past week. Three families. Six adults, five kids. Might have been named Eckert?"

"They was here," he said. "I never got no name."

"They were?" This was much easier than he'd thought it would be. "When?"

"Like you said—well, maybe not week—five days ago, maybe."

"Did you have occasion to talk to them?"

"I talked to a couple of the men," Hacker said. "They left their rigs out in back of my place, and I took care of the horses."

"Did they stay in a hotel?"

"Yeah, they spent one night in the New Hope Hotel. One of the newer places in town."

"They had the money for that?"

"They had plenty of money, and like blamed-fool Easterners, they was flashin' it. I'm surprised they got outta town in one piece."

"They got out that way," Clint said, "but they didn't stay that way."

"Huh?"

"They're dead?"

"All of 'em?" Hacker asked. "Even the kids?"

"That's right."

"How's that happen?"

"Somebody killed them."

"Jesus."

"What were they doing here, Jim?"

"They was askin' about Mr. Sutcliffe."

"Who's he?"

"Grant Sutcliffe. He's a businessman in town. Owns a lot of property."

"You know what they wanted with him?"

"Somethin' about some property, I think," Hacker said. "One of the little boys kept askin' his father when they was gonna get to their new home."

"Tell me about Sutcliffe. Is he honest?"

"He's in business," Hacker said, "and he's good at it. Ain't nobody like that honest—not total."

"You do business with him?"

"Hell no. This place is mine, free and clear. I ain't partners with them."

"Them?"

"Him and his partner," Hacker said.

"And who's that?"

"Harry Cantrell."

"And he's not honest at all, right?"

"What makes ya say that?"

"Just the way you say his name."

"Well, let's just say he has a reputation for gettin' what he wants."

"Were those families in his way?"

"That I don't know."

"But you do know where I can find Mr. Sutcliffe and his partner, Mr. Cantrell?"

"I can tell you where Sutcliffe is," Hacker said. "You'll hafta find Cantrell through him."

"Good enough, Jim." He took out some money.

"Ya ain't gotta pay me, Mr. Adams," Hacker said. "Them kids was cute. If I can help ya find out who killed 'em, I will."

"Thanks, Jim."

He told Clint where to find Grant Sutcliffe.

SIXTEEN

Clint followed Jim Hacker's directions to Grant Sutcliffe's office. His name was on the door, but not what kind of business he was in. He thought about knocking, but he could see through the glass there was a man seated at a desk. He opened the door and entered.

"Can I help you?" the man asked.

"Sutcliffe?"

"I'm Grant Sutcliffe," the man said, standing. "What can I do for you?"

"My name's Clint Adams," Clint said. "I'd like to ask you a few questions about some people who were here in Roswell about a week ago."

"What makes you think I know anything that would help you?"

"Because when they came to town they asked for you."

"Okay, so they asked for me," Sutcliffe said. "Maybe

they even came to talk to me. Why do I have to discuss that with you?"

"You don't. The family name was Eckert. At least, one of their names was Eckert."

"Eckert," Sutcliffe repeated. "Eckert . . . wait a minute, yes. I do remember."

"How could you not? Three families in three wagons—" Clint started.

"Excuse me," Sutcliffe said, sitting down, "but I only spoke to one man. I believe his name was Eckert."

"And what did he want?"

"He wanted to buy some land."

"And?"

"I didn't have any to sell him."

"And they went on their way?"

"They did."

"But they went north," Clint said. "If you didn't have any land to sell them, why didn't they head south? Back the way came?"

"I don't know," Sutcliffe said. "I couldn't say."

"Did Mr. Eckert talk to your partner?" Clint asked. "Mr. Cantrell?"

"How do you know—well, yes, I think Harry was here, at that time."

"And where is he now?"

"I suppose he's in Carrizozo. That's where his main office is."

"Did he speak to Mr. Eckert?"

"I think I handled the whole negotiation."

"It doesn't sound like there was much of a negotiation."

"No, you're right, there wasn't."

"You don't seem to have a very clear memory of something that happened only days ago, Mr. Sutcliffe. I've been told that you're a good businessman."

"Who told you that?"

"Word gets around," Clint said. "Sometimes you don't even have to ask."

Sutcliffe frowned.

"I don't think I like the idea of people in town talking about me."

"That's what comes from being a success, isn't it?" Clint asked.

"I suppose so."

"Can you tell me when Mr. Cantrell will be back here, Mr. Sutcliffe?"

"Next month."

"Not before then?"

"Unless there's some sort of emergency, he only comes into once a month so we can go over the books."

"I see," Clint said. "So he's the senior partner?"

"We're equal partners."

"Does he know that?"

"Mr. Adams," Sutcliffe said, "is there anything else I can do for you?"

"I need your opinion on something."

"What's that?"

"Why do you suppose," Clint asked, "Mr. Eckert and his entire family were killed?"

"Killed?" Sutcliffe repeated. "What do you mean, killed?"

"Just what I said," Clint said. "I came across their camp, and they were all dead."

"That's terrible. How were they killed?"

"Hard to tell," Clint said. "Right now the general opinion is that they were poisoned."

"Poisoned?"

"The whole family, including the children."

"Who would—"

"That's what I'm asking," Clint said, walking to the door, "and that's what I intend to find out."

SEVENTEEN

Clint was sitting in the Red Sand Saloon when Sheriff Turner walked in. There wasn't much business, and he'd taken a table near the back. The lawman spotted him and walked directly to his table.

"I thought you were gonna stay out of trouble?" he said.

"I think I have," Clint said. "If you think different, have a seat and a drink and tell me about it."

"You want another beer?" Turner asked.

"No, I'll finish this one. Sit down, though. I owe you a drink."

The lawman sat. Clint went to the bar and came back with a beer.

"There you go," Clint said, seating himself again. "Now tell me, what have I done?"

"You bothered one of this town's leading citizens," Turner said.

"Sutcliffe?"

Turner nodded.

"He made a complaint?"

"No," Turner said, "but I know just the same that you went to talk to him."

"How's that starting trouble?"

"We like for our leading citizens to be happy," Turner said.

"Did I make him unhappy?"

"I don't know," Turner said. "I don't even know what the two of you talked about. I just want you to stay away from him."

"No problem."

"You mean you will?"

"Sure," Clint said. "I'm probably leaving town tomorrow."

"Oh," Turner said.

"Disappointed that you won't have time to run me out?" Clint asked.

"I'd hate to try it," Turner said. "But I would if I had to."

"You don't have to."

"That's fine."

"You could tell me something, though, before I leave."

"What's that?"

"Do you know who killed those families?"

"Adams—"

"Are you covering for somebody?"

"Like who?"

"Like one of your leading citizens?"

"You think Mr. Sutcliffe killed them?"

"No, not him," Clint said. "I don't think he's got it in him."

"Then you think he had it done?"

"Or somebody else did," Clint said.

"Like?"

"What's Harry Cantrell like?"

"He's a ruthless businessman," the sheriff said, "but what reason would he have to kill three families?"

"I don't know," Clint said. "Maybe I'll have to go to Carrizozo and ask him."

"I wouldn't advise that," Turner said.

"Why not?"

"He's not like Sutcliffe."

"So I understand," Clint said, "you're saying he'd send somebody after me?"

"I'm not sayin' that," Turner replied, "but if he did, it wouldn't be somebody you could just shrug off. It'd be the best money can buy."

"Well, if he did that, that would be like admitting he had those people killed, wouldn't it?"

"Uh, no—"

"Don't worry, Sheriff," Clint said. "I'll give him a chance to explain. And I'll tell him you tried to do your job and warn me off."

"Adams," Turner said, "this doesn't make sense. What makes you think he's even in—"

"They came to town and spoke to him and Sutcliffe," Clint said. "Right?"

"I suppose—"

"Anybody else?"

"Not that I know of," the sheriff said. "A desk clerk—"

"But nobody like those two, right? No other important citizens of Roswell??

"No."

"Well then, I've already talked to Sutcliffe," Clint said, "that only leaves me Cantrell. Why would he mind talking to me if he hasn't done anything?"

"I don't know, Adams," Sheriff Turner said, resignedly, "but I guess you're gonna find out, ain'tcha?"

"I guess I am."

EIGHTEEN

Johnny Devlin rode into Carrizozo and went directly to the office of Harry Cantrell. Once they'd dragged him out of the whorehouse and got him to clean himself up, he'd mounted right up and rode out.

It was dark by the time he got to town. The front door of Cantrell's office was locked, but he knew where his boss lived. He mounted up and rode over to Cantrell's big house.

Cantrell rolled the woman over on her belly, grabbed her hips, and hiked her butt up.

"I'm going to stick you in your butt, Ava," he said, rubbing her ass lovingly.

"That's gonna cost extra, Mr. Cantrell," the woman told him.

"That doesn't matter," he said. "I've got extra, you know that."

She wiggled her pale, naked butt at him and said, "You pay, you can do what you want."

Cantrell got off the bed, retrieved his wallet from the nearby dresser, took out some money, and let the bills rain down on the naked girl's body.

"That enough?"

"For you to pork me in the ass?" Ava asked, laughing. "That's plenty, lover."

Cantrell got back on the bed, spread her cheeks, pressed the head of his engorged prick to her anus and was prepared to push when there was an insistent knocking at his door.

"Fuck!"

"Who the hell is that at this time, Harry?" Ava demanded.

"I don't know!"

"Well find out, and make them go away," she said, turning over so he could see her melon-sized, brown-nippled breasts. Actually, these days they were more pear-shaped than melon, the way they were when he first married her fifteen years ago.

The knock came again and Ava complained, "They're ruinin' the game, Harry! You wanna fuck my ass, you better get rid of them."

"Yeah, yeah," he said.

He left the bedroom, grabbing a robe as he went. He was belting it as he approached the front door. He was surprised to see Devlin standing there when he swung it open.

"What the hell are you doing here, Johnny?" he demanded.

"Sheriff Turner sent me, Mr. Cantrell."

"What for?"

"To warn you."

"About what?"

"Clint Adams."

Cantrell frowned. "What's the Gunsmith got to do with me?" he demanded.

"I don't know," Devlin said. "He just wanted me to come here and tell you that Adams was in Roswell, askin' questions."

"About what?"

"You know," Devlin said, "about those folks."

"Why didn't he just send a telegram?"

"I dunno—"

Cantrell knew. Turner was being careful. Telegrams could be read by somebody other than the key operator and the recipient.

"Why the hell is the Gunsmith interested in those people?" he said aloud.

"I dunno, Mr.—"

"I'm not asking you!" Cantrell snapped. "Okay, you delivered your message. Now go away."

"Where?" Devlin asked. "Should I go on back to Roswell?"

Cantrell was about to say yes, but stopped himself.

"No," he said, "get a hotel room in town. A cheap one. Tomorrow, find me Eddie Pratt, and some of his men."

"Pratt?"

"That's right. You know him, right?"

Devlin swallowed. "Yeah, I know him." And he was afraid of him.

"Just tell him I need him. Tell him to come to my office and see me."

"You gonna use him and his guns—"

"Don't ask any questions, Johnny," Cantrell said. "Don't try to think. You'll just strain yourself."

"Yessir, Mr. Cantrell."

"Come and see me after you find Pratt."

"Yessir."

"Now go on!"

Devlin nodded, and backed away from the door.

Cantrell closed the door and locked it, stood there for a moment, thinking. What possible connection could those people have had to the Gunsmith? His involvement was not good news, but Cantrell always thought he had enough money to overcome anything.

The Gunsmith should be no different.

He turned and went back to the bedroom.

"Who the hell was that?" Ava asked. She was sitting up on the bed, still naked, picking at her toes. Cantrell wondered when she had become such a disgusting slag? He liked having her on all fours. Her backside was still firm, and her skin still smooth. It was only when she turned over that he saw what the years had done to her.

"Johnny Devlin."

"Devlin." She took her hands away from her feet and wrapped them around her knees. "A whore once told me he has a huge dick, a gorgeous one, but that he doesn't know what to do with it."

"Ava—"

"Luckily," she said, reaching into his robe and grabbed his prick, "you don't have the same problem."

"Ava, I can't now," he said. "I've got other things on my mind."

"Oh no," she said, yanking on him, "you don't get to take care of those things until you take care of what's on my mind."

Slag or no slag, when she took hold of him and talked to him like that he started to get hard again.

"Maybe you need some help first?" she asked.

She got off the bed, stripped the robe off of him, then got down on her knees in front of him and took him into her mouth.

"Oh yeah . . ." he said, forgetting all about Johnny Devlin, Clint Adams, and dead families for the time being . . .

NINETEEN

While he ate breakfast, Clint thought over his decision, and the logic it had been based on.

If you could call it logic.

All he had to go on was what the old-timer from the livery told him, and his own instincts about Grant Sutcliffe—not to mention Sheriff Turner.

It seemed like Harry Cantrell was the man they all looked to. If a decision had been made to kill eleven people, it would have come from him.

Clint paid for his breakfast and left the café. He walked to the livery to retrieve Eclipse.

"Takin' him out this time?" Jim Hacker asked.

"Afraid so," Clint said. "I'm done here."

"Find out what you needed to?"

"I think I found out where to go to find out what I need to know," Clint said. "Who do you know in Carrizozo?"

"Feller name Jenkins runs a livery stable there. He'll take good care of your horse."

"And give me some information?"

"He's like me," Hacker said. "Keeps his ears open."

"That's good enough," Clint said. "Saddle him up, will you?"

"Sure."

"Thanks."

Clint waited outside. When Hacker walked Eclipse out, he asked Clint, "You want me to send Jenkins a telegram?"

"No," Clint said, "somebody else might read it."

"I get ya. Here ya go." He handed over Eclipse's reins. "Bring him back anytime."

"Yeah," Clint said, doubting he'd ever be back.

He mounted up, gave old Jim a wave, and rode off.

He was riding down Main Street when the sheriff came out of his office. He veered toward the lawman.

"On your way?"

"Yep."

"Comin' back?"

"Not if I don't have to."

"Watch yourself."

"Did you send a telegram to Cantrell?" Clint asked.

"Why would I do that?" the lawman asked.

"To keep one of your solid citizens happy."

Turner looked away. "No, I didn't send a telegram."

No, Clint thought, you probably sent a rider. Which meant Cantrell would be waiting for him.

He needed to send a telegram from somewhere between Roswell and Carrizozo. There must be a town with a telegraph line in that eighty or so miles.

"Thanks for the help, Sheriff," he said. "Don't expect I'll be seeing you again."

Unless, of course, he found out that the lawman had something to do with killing those people. Then he'd be back with a federal marshal.

Once Clint Adams had ridden out of town, Sheriff Turner crossed the street and walked down to the telegraph office. He hated to do it, but he knew who buttered his bread.

"Sheriff," the clerk said.

He hastily scribbled and note and said, "Send this right away to Carrizozo, Len."

TWENTY

Clint could have ridden into Carrizozo late that evening, but he decided to camp within spitting distance of the town.

He'd found the telegraph line he'd been looking for in a town called Lester and sent a telegram to Sheriff Scott in Hondo. He got an answer back within the hour. It was what he needed to know.

He built a fire and made some coffee, used it to wash down some beef jerky.

The sheriff in Carrizozo was named Glenister and, according to Sheriff Scott, he was his own man. Clint was going to take that information with a grain of salt. Too many lawmen who started out as their own men had succumbed to men with money. And judging by everything he'd learned, Cantrell had a lot of it.

He'd stop in and see Sheriff Glenister in the morning, make his own judgment about the man before going any further.

* * *

Clint broke camp in the morning and saddled up. He'd be getting into Carrizozo early enough to get some breakfast there. He tried always to take care of his stomach, because he needed to be alert at all times.

Carrizozo had all the earmarks of a growing town, not the last of which was the scent of newly cut wood in the air. There were new buildings on both sides of the street, some of them two stories high. He picked out a hotel for himself, then went in search of the livery and Old Jim's pal Jenkins.

When he found the livery a tall, skinny fellow stopped what he was doing to watch Clint ride Eclipse in.

"Good God, fella," the man said, "now that's a horse!"

"You Jenkins?" Clint asked.

"I'm Lou Jenkins, yeah," the man said, staring at Clint owlishly. He had one eye that seemed to open only halfway. Clint guessed him to be somewhere in his sixties.

"Jim Hacker said I could count on you," Clint said, dismounting.

"For what?" Jenkins asked, suspiciously.

"Well, to take care of my horse, for one."

"That I can and will do, gladly. What else?"

"Information."

"About what?"

"Anything."

"You want a bartender for that, Mister."

"Bartenders listen real well," Clint said, "but they also talk a lot. I don't want anybody knowing my business."

Jenkins rubbed a big hand over his long jaw, making a scratching sound as he did it.

"I can pay," Clint said.

"That ain't the issue," Jenkins said.

"What is, then?" Clint asked.

"Stayin' alive."

"You don't even know who or what I'm interested in, yet."

"Mister," Jenkins said. "I can tell by lookin' at you that you ain't about to ask questions about the local preacher. What's your name, anyway?"

"Clint Adams."

Jenkins pointed at him and said, "See? You're lookin' for trouble, ain'tcha?"

"I'm afraid I am, Lou," Clint said. "Trouble named Harry Cantrell."

Jenkins stared at him, then put his hand out.

"Hand over your horse," Jenkins said, "and tell me what you want to know."

"Cantrell is a ruthless sonofabitch," Jenkins said as he rubbed Eclipse down. "You goin' up against him, you better have one of two things on your side."

"What's that?"

"The law, or a fast gun."

"I just might have both."

"Then you just might be able to take him on," Jenkins said. "What is it you think he's done?"

"I think he might have killed eleven people," Clint said. "Six adults, five children."

"Kids?"

Clint nodded.

"That's bad business, killin' kids."

"That the kind of thing you think he could do?" Clint asked.

"If they was in his way," Jenkins said, "he'd kill his own ma and pa—if they was still alive."

"Does he have any family?" Clint asked.

"Just a wife."

"What's she like?"

"From what I hear, she's got the appetite of a whore," Jenkins said. "That might make some men happy, but she also looks like an old whore."

"That's the word going around?" Clint asked.

"On her, yeah."

"Does the man have regular guns he employs?"

"He needs a gun, he gets the best available," Jenkins said. "Whoever's around. If he knew you was around, he'd probably try to hire you."

"Too late for that," Clint said. "I'm pretty sure he already knows I'm coming."

"If that's the case," Jenkins said, "you better watch your back."

TWENTY-ONE

Cantrell looked up when his office door opened and Eddie Pratt entered, followed by Johnny Devlin.

"Here he is, Mr. Cantrell," Devlin said.

"I can see that, Johnny. Have a seat, Eddie. I may have a job for you that you'll find very interesting."

"I hope you ain't gonna ask me to satisfy your wife," Pratt said. "I don't think I'm up to it."

Devlin snickered and Cantrell said, "Get out, Devlin!"

"Yes, sir."

Cantrell looked at Pratt. The gunman was in his thirties, tall and rangy and, as usual, abrasive.

"Why do you insist on talking about my wife like that?" he demanded.

"She's a damn slut," Pratt said. "Everybody in town knows that. Want me to kill 'er for you?"

Cantrell stared at Pratt for a few moments, then grinned and said, "Don't tempt me. Get yourself a drink and sit down."

"Naw," Pratt said, "all you got is that brandy swill. I'll sit, though." And he did. "What's on your mind?"

"How'd you like to enhance your reputation?" Cantrell asked.

"I wouldn't," Pratt said.

"Why not?"

"Because I ain't got one, you know that," Pratt said. "I try to keep a low profile. I do my job, and get paid. I don't wanna make a big name for myself."

"Okay, then," Cantrell said, "how'd you like to make three times your normal fee?"

"Uh-oh."

"What?"

"You got a bad one on your hands, Cantrell, or you wouldn't be offerin' me that much money."

Cantrell didn't respond.

"Okay, so who is it?" Pratt asked.

"The Gunsmith."

Pratt looked surprised.

"Clint Adams is in town?"

"That's right."

"Lookin' for you."

"Right."

"What's it about?"

"Those settlers."

"That was a bad business," Pratt said. "I knew that wasn't a good idea."

"I had no choice," Cantrell said. "They had legal deeds. They had to go."

"Well," Pratt said, "I don't want any part of Clint Adams. Not for five times the price. Not if you want me to take him face to face."

"What if I said you could take him any way you want?" Cantrell asked.

"Well," Pratt said, "that would be different. When do you want it done?"

"Next couple of days," Cantrell said. "I don't want him killed the day he arrives, asking about me."

"That makes sense," Pratt said. "I'll need some help, though."

"Three times as much for them, too?" Cantrell asked, standing up and turning to his safe.

"No," Pratt said, "regular price for them."

Cantrell nodded, knelt in front of his safe, and opened it.

"Five times the price for me," Pratt said.

Cantrell paused, then said over his shoulder, "Four?"

"Okay," Pratt said, "but only because you're a good customer."

Cantrell took out the money, stuffed it into an envelope, and handed it to Pratt.

"Can I use Devlin?" he asked.

"The man's an idiot," Cantrell said, seating himself again.

"Then he'll come cheap," Pratt said. "I won't give him anything important to do."

"Very well," Cantrell said. "He's yours. Tell him I said so."

Pratt grinned, stowed the envelope inside his jacket, and headed for the door.

"Pratt."

The gunman turned.

"You'd really do it?"

"Do what?"

"Kill my wife?"

"Sure."

Cantrell sat back, considering the offer.

Pratt opened the door, then turned and looked back at Cantrell. "For five times the price," he said, and stepped outside, pulling the door closed behind him.

TWENTY-TWO

Clint was meeting a lot of new lawmen lately.

Glenister turned out to be a man who looked too big to ever get into the saddle again. He had his boots off and was rubbing his feet when Clint entered. There were holes in his socks.

"Sorry," he said. "Not a dignified way for you to find the sheriff, eh?" He laughed.

"Hey, when your feet hurt you've got to rub them, right?"

"Just give me a minute to get these boots back on," Glenister said, struggling with them. "Ah, hell, you might as well tell me who you are and what you want while I'm doin' this."

"My name's Clint Adams," he said. "And I'm looking for a killer."

"In my town?"

"I hope so," Clint said. "I've been to Hondo, Roswell, and now here."

Glenister got his boots on and straightened up, sweating from the effort.

"I need a beer," he said. "Come on. Let's go to the saloon and you can tell me all about why the Gunsmith is lookin' for a killer in my town."

The sheriff took Clint to a saloon called the Three-Leaf Clover. Business was slow at that time of day and they stood at the bar with cold beers in their hands.

"Okay," Glenister said. "Tell me."

Clint laid it out for the lawman, right up to his suspicion that Harry Cantrell had something to do with it.

"Sheriff Scott in Hondo tells me that you are your own man," Clint finished, "and that I don't have to worry about you running to him to tell him about me."

"I won't have to," Glenister said. "He probably knows by now. He's got enough eyes and ears in this town without me."

"I see."

"What do you plan to do?"

"Talk to him."

"Confront him?"

"Not exactly," Clint said. "First I'll just ask him if he knows the families. See how he reacts."

"Badly," Glenister said. "He'll react badly."

"Well, I'd expect that," Clint said. "And once I do accuse him . . ."

"If he did it," Glenister said, "he'll try to kill you. If he didn't do it . . . well, he may still try to have you killed."

"I'll take my chances."

"I've got four deputies, Adams," Glenister said. "If you

do find a murderer in this town—whether it's Cantrell or somebody else—we're at your disposal."

"I appreciate that, Sheriff."

"When are you gonna see Cantrell?"

"As soon as I finish this beer," Clint said. "Can you direct me to his office?"

"I'll point the way," the lawman said.

The door to Cantrell's office opened again a half-hour later. This time a man he'd never seen before entered. He assumed it was Clint Adams.

"Mr. Cantrell?"

"That's right," Cantrell said. "Can I help you?"

"My name is Clint Adams."

"Should that mean something— Oh, wait. I know. The Gunsmith, right?"

"That's right."

"Well, come in," Cantrell said. "Have a seat and tell me what's on your mind. Can I offer you some brandy?"

"No, I'm fine." Clint sat across from the man.

"What brings you to Carrizozo, Mr. Adams?" Cantrell asked. "Or, more to the point, what brings you to me?"

"Actually," Clint said, "murder."

"Murder?" Cantrell looked confused. "Has someone I know been murdered?"

"You know a family named Eckert?"

"Eckert." Cantrell seemed to think. "Doesn't ring a bell with me."

"Six adults, five children."

"Was this Mr. Eckert killed?"

"They were all killed," Clint told him.

"All?"

"That's right."

"Even the children?"

"That's right."

"That's terrible."

"Yes, it is," Clint agreed.

"But why does this bring you to me?" Cantrell asked.

Clint grinned and said, "That is the question, isn't it?"

TWENTY-THREE

"Are you going to answer it?"

"I found these families dead on the trail," Clint said, "in camp. I backtracked and followed their tracks to Roswell."

"Why did you do that?" Cantrell asked. "Are you a lawman?"

"No," Clint said, "I'm a responsible man. I found them, so I want to find out who killed them."

"And did you find out?"

"No," Clint said, "but I did discover that they had talked to a man named Sutcliffe—and to you."

"Did they?" Cantrell said. "I'll have to check with Grant to find out what it was about."

"You don't remember?"

"I don't have a very good memory—"

"I thought you needed to, in order to be a good businessman."

"—about some things," Cantrell finished.

"Not people?"

"Important people, yes."

"Will you remember me, after today?" Clint asked.

"Should I?"

"Oh yes," Clint said, "I think you should, Mr. Cantrell. I definitely think you should." He stood up.

"We'll be talking again."

"Anything I can do to help," Cantrell said. He stood and extended his hand. Clint ignored it, turned, and walked to the door.

"I'll be calling on you, Mr. Cantrell."

"I'll be waiting, Mr. Adams."

They sized each other up again, and then Clint left.

Cantrell sat back in his chair, uncomfortably. He was glad he had already sent for Eddie Pratt.

"So I'm supposed to work for you?" Devlin asked Pratt.

"That's right."

"Mr. Cantrell says so?"

"You can check with him if you want," Pratt said. He put some money on the table. It was nothing to him, but a lot to Johnny Devlin.

"No," Devlin said, "that's okay. Whaddaya want me to do, Eddie?"

"I haven't decided yet," Pratt said, "but for now you can get us a couple of beers."

"Sure."

Devlin stood up and waited. Apparently, he didn't want to use his newfound fortune to pay for the beer. Pratt gave him some more money.

As Devlin went to the bar, Pratt looked around the saloon. The place catered mostly to locals, of the type he was looking for: men who would do anything for money. But he didn't just need greedy men, he needed men with a talent for violence.

Devlin came back with the beers.

"Johnny, do you know Elton Brand?"

"Yeah, I know Elton."

"Can you find him?"

"Sure. Are you gonna hire him?"

"I am."

"You can get somebody in here a lot cheaper," Devlin pointed out.

"I may just do that," Pratt said, "but I'll also need Brand."

"Okay." Devlin took two swallows of beer.

"Now, Johnny," Pratt said. "Go and find Elton now."

Devlin stared down at his beer, quickly took two more swallows, then said, "Sure," and hurried for the door.

Pratt sat back with his beer and continued to look over the local talent.

Clint left Cantrell's office and walked back toward the sheriff's office. The lawman was standing out in front, watching him approach.

"Had your meetin'?" Glenister asked.

"I have."

"How did it go?"

"I think we both understood each other."

"If he understood you," Glenister said, "then he's probably gonna try to kill you."

"Tell me something, Sheriff."

"If I can."

"Why would a successful man like Harry Cantrell want to kill six adults and five children?"

Glenister rubbed his jowls. "I can only think of one reason."

"And what's that?"

"Profit."

"Exactly what I was thinking. Now all I have to do is find out how he profits from their death."

TWENTY-FOUR

As Clint was about to walk away the sheriff asked, "Think it would help you to talk to another partner of Cantrell's?"

"I think that would help a lot," Clint said, "but why would one of his other partners talk to me?"

"Because this one became partners against her will."

"A woman?"

Glenister nodded. "And a widow. When her husband died, she discovered that he had become partners with Cantrell. So, if she wanted to stay in business, she had to stay partners with him."

"And you think she'll talk to me?"

"Oh yeah," Glenister said, "she'll talk to you."

"Okay, then."

"Her name's Lisa Mason," the Sheriff said.

"What's her business? Saloon? Hotel?"

"Mercantile," Glenister said, "and Gun Shop."

"Gun Shop?"

"Her husband was a gunsmith."

*   *   *

Clint tried the mercantile first, was told by the clerk behind the counter that Mrs. Mason was at the "Gun Shop."

"Used to be called the Gunsmith Shop, but she changed it after her Mister died," the man said. "She ain't no gunsmith."

"I see," Clint said. "Thanks."

He got directions from the man and walked over to the Gun Shop.

The Gun Shop was off the main street, a large store with two windows filled with guns. On closer inspection, Clint saw that one window had new guns, and the other some recycled weapons.

As he entered the store the top of the door struck a small bell, sending out a warning tinkle.

"I'm in the back!" a woman's voice shouted. "Look around."

He did. Most of the guns in the place were under glass, but there were a few retooled old rifles that were available to be hefted and aimed. He was doing so when she came out.

She was a tall woman with red hair piled atop her head, some tendrils of which had come loose and were hanging down in her face. Her solid body was packed into a man's shirt and some jeans. She had pale skin which, upon closer look, had a spray of just visible freckles across the bridge of her nose, and cheeks—along with a smear of gun oil. Her eyes were green and curious and she regarded him. She was a mature woman, probably close to forty.

"Help ya?" she asked.

"I was hoping to talk to you," he said. "The sheriff told me we might help each other."

"And did he say how?" she asked. He noticed her hands were dirty with dust and gun oil.

"Maybe I should introduce myself first," he suggested.

"Why don't you tell me what it's about first, and then we'll see if an introduction is necessary," she countered.

"Harry Cantrell."

She narrowed her eyes. "You work for him?"

"On the contrary," he said. "I'm pretty sure I'm going to try to prove he's a murderer."

"Flip that OPEN sign in the window around to the CLOSED side, and let's talk," she said.

TWENTY-FIVE

"Shall I introduce myself?" he asked.

"Not that it matters," she said. "If you're tryin' to put Cantrell away, I'm your girl."

"My name's Clint Adams."

Her mouth fell open, but then she recovered and closed it. She also tried to tuck those tendrils of hair back up, but they wouldn't stay.

"I'm, uh, a mess," she stammered, "I, um, was in the back—"

"It's okay, Mrs. Mason."

"My husband would be thrilled to know you're in his shop."

"It's an interesting-looking place. Lots of wall space—"

"I always asked him why he didn't put some guns on the walls!" she said. "He always liked to keep the guns under glass."

"Keeps them cleaner," Clint said.

"I suppose. I put those rifles out, but I figure anybody

who buys a gun is going to clean it anyway. Am I right?"

"They should," Clint said, "that doesn't mean they do."

She was still standing in the middle of the store, fussing with her hair.

"Am I making you uncomfortable?"

"No," she said, annoyed, "I'm making myself uncomfortable. Why don't you come to the back with me? I can offer you a drink."

"Thanks."

He followed her through a doorway, watching the way her buttocks moved in her jeans.

"That's storage," she said, pointing. "That's where I was when you came in. I have an office in here, though."

They went through another door, into a small room with a desk and a couple of chairs.

"I have some whiskey," she said, seating herself behind a desk and producing a bottle and two glasses.

"That's fine," he said.

She poured a couple of fingers into the two glasses and handed him one.

"To your late husband," he said.

"He was a hard man to live with," she said.

"Okay then," he said, "to you."

"What for?"

"For successfully having two businesses going," Clint said.

"Not like I could do it without—"

"Just drink."

"Yeah okay."

They sipped whiskey.

"Sorry," she said. "I guess the answer to your last

question is yes, you're making me uncomfortable, and not just a little nervous."

"Why?"

"You have a reputation," she said. "And you're the Gunsmith. *And* we're in my gun shop, such as it is."

"I understand your husband was a gunsmith?"

"Yes, he knew a lot about guns," she said. "I just sell 'em, don't know that much about them."

"That's gun oil on your hand—and cheek, by the way."

"Oh." She swiped at her face, just managed to smear it even further. "I was moving some gun oil in the back."

She tried to wipe her hands on her jeans, then used her sleeve to try to clean her face.

"Forget it," Clint said, laughing. "You can do it in front of a mirror later."

She sipped her drink and said, "Why don't you tell me what you think you have on Cantrell?"

He did. Took a sip of his own drink, then launched into his explanation, starting when he found the dead people in their camp.

"Children?" she asked. "They killed children?"

Clint nodded. "Is that something you can see Harry Cantrell doing?" he asked.

"Oh, yeah," she said. "Harry will do anything if he thinks he can make a profit from it."

"That's what the sheriff told me," Clint said. "So what I have to figure is how he benefits from killing those families."

"Why would three families come out West like that, with everything they own?"

"To settle," he said.

"And what would they need in order to settle?"

He could tell from the look on her face that she was just throwing out questions, without knowing the answers. Clint thought a moment, then said, "Land."

"Yes!" she said. "Most of Harry's holdings are land."

Clint sat forward excitedly. "What if those families came out here to settle, and already had their land."

"Deeds in hand," she said.

"They talked in Roswell to Cantrell and his partner Sutcliffe."

"They would have gone to them with their deeds," she said, "wanting to take possession of their property."

"And what if Cantrell wanted that property?"

"So he offers to buy it from them."

"They refused."

"So he decided to kill them."

"The doctor in Hondo thinks they were poisoned," Clint said. "He can't prove it until he gets the results of some tests from Santa Fe."

"How do you poison eleven people?" she asked.

"You put it in their food, or water supply," Clint said.

"He has plenty of men working for him who'd do it, too," she said.

Clint had put his empty glass down on the desk. Lisa leaned forward and poured more whiskey into his glass, then into her own.

"That sonofabitch!" she hissed. "If we could prove this I could get out from under him."

"That's what I'm going to try to do," Clint said, "prove it."

"I'll do everything I can to help," she said.

"Now all we have to do is figure out what that would be."

TWENTY-SIX

"How do you get along with Cantrell?"

"I force myself to," she said. "I hate him, but it wouldn't do me any good to let him see that."

"Anything else?"

"Yes," she said, squirming in her seat, "whenever I'm in the same room with him I feel like he's looking right through my clothes. It makes me feel . . . dirty."

"I understand he's married?"

"Oh, now there's a winner," she said. "His wife is a pig, in more ways than one. She's supposed to be very talented."

"In what way?"

"You know." She squirmed again. "I mean . . . sex."

"And you know this how?"

"She's had other men in town besides her husband," Lisa said, "and they talk."

"So she's not an attractive woman?"

"No," Lisa said, "but I've heard that men have said

that doesn't matter once you are in bed with her."

Clint himself had been with women, who, while not gorgeous, had been very good in bed, but he had to admit he had not been with a woman who simply was not attractive. Maybe he'd been missing something all these years.

Lisa had some more whiskey, and when she spoke he thought he could detect a slur of her words.

"If Cantrell's getting such good sex at home, why's he always leering at me?" she wondered.

"I can understand that," Clint said. "You're a beautiful woman."

"Ha," she said. "If I wasn't a widow, folks would be callin' me an old maid."

"There's nothing old maidish about you, believe me, Lisa. Can I call you Lisa?"

"Sure, you can," she said. "Old maidish?" She giggled. "Is that even a word?"

"Maybe I made it up," he said.

She finished her drink, and reached for the bottle. Clint quickly grabbed it before she could.

"I think we've had enough whiskey," he said.

"Huh?"

"I get the feeling you don't drink all that much, Lisa."

"Once in a while," she admitted.

"Listen," he said, "why don't we go someplace and get some coffee?"

"And some food?" she asked, eyes widening. "I'm really hungry."

"Sure," he said. "It's time for dinner anyway, right?"

She slapped her desk with her palms and said, "Let's go. There's a place right down the street."

* * *

Add one more to the countless small cafes Clint had been to, in towns all over the West. It was much the same, too. Great smells, a small amount of tables, a waiter and a waitress hustling around the room carrying plates.

"Come on," Lisa said, grabbing his sleeve, "they always keep a table open for me. I eat here all the time."

She tugged him across the room to an empty table. Luckily, it was in the back and he was able to sit against a wall.

"Hey, Lisa," the waitress said. She was about Lisa's age, but looked older. She had probably been waiting tables for years. "Who's your friend?"

"Meet, Clint Adams, Milly," Lisa said. "He's gonna help me get—"

"—some good guns for her store," Clint said, cutting her off.

"Oh, well that's good," the waitress said. "What'll you folks have?"

"Can I order?" Lisa asked Clint.

"Sure, why not? It's your town."

"Two beef stew specials, Milly."

"Comin' up."

"And coffee," I said.

"Right away."

She went away to place their orders, then came back with a big pot and two cups. She poured each a cup, then left the pot.

Clint hoped that the food and coffee would help Lisa Mason sober up. He also hoped the woman wouldn't feel too embarrassed about having gotten herself drunk.

"Thank you," she said, then.

"For what?"

"For taking the whiskey bottle away," she said. "For taking me out to eat something. For keeping me from making a fool of myself."

Clint didn't know quite that to say, so he just said, "You're welcome."

TWENTY-SEVEN

When they were finished, Lisa didn't want to go to the Gun Shop or the mercantile. She asked Clint if he would walk her home.

She lived in a residential section of the town, with neighbors close on either side as well as across the street.

"I lived in this house with my husband for ten years," she said. "Now I've been here three years without him."

As they entered the house, he could see it had a distinct feminine feel to it.

"I changed a lot after he died," she said. "He was . . . overbearing, wouldn't let me do anything with the house. So after he died I just changed everything."

"It's nice," Clint said. "It feels homey."

"Thank you. I can make coffee if you want to keep talking? About Cantrell, I mean?"

"Uh, sure, why not?" He had the feeling she didn't want him to leave. Maybe there was something she'd been wanting to tell him, but hadn't gotten to it yet.

"Make yourself comfortable," she said. "I'll make the coffee and bring it out here."

Clint sat on the sofa and continued to look around at the living room. Everything reflected Lisa's taste which, while feminine, was not girly.

He soon became impatient, realizing that he should have been out taking some sort of action rather than just sitting here. He was about to go into the kitchen to tell her he had to leave when she appeared with a tray bearing a coffeepot and cups.

"I don't have many people here to the house," she said, putting the tray down on the table in front of the sofa. "This will be nice."

"Yes," he said, "it will."

He didn't have the heart to leave now so he allowed her to pour, and then she sat next to him.

This was the closest he had been to her all afternoon and he realized he could smell her. It was a heady scent and it was all hers, nothing artificial. As she turned to smile at him he saw something else. Her eyes seemed to be on fire, and her nostrils were flaring.

She was in heat, and the smell of her was starting to arouse him.

She wasn't drunk, though. The food and coffee had taken care of that. If anything happened, he wouldn't feel he was taking advantage of her.

It was getting late in the day; there wasn't much time to do anything else. He decided to sit back, enjoy the coffee and the company.

They started talking about her business. "Actually, since my husband died, my businesses have been doing pretty well," she said.

"Maybe that's why Harry Cantrell wants to keep his piece," Clint said.

"I don't know why Andy—my husband—even went to Cantrell for help. I think he just panicked when things got kind of rough. I told him we could ride it out, but he never gave my opinions any weight."

"That's too bad," Clint said. "He didn't realize how smart you are."

"I think," she said, "he was worried I was smarter than he was."

"So it was all about ego."

"Oh yes," she said. "He had this image of himself as a businessman, and he just wasn't."

"Can you buy Cantrell out?"

"No," she said. "I'm doing okay, but I don't have that kind of money." She put her hand on his arm. "If you can prove he killed those people, I'd be rid of him. In fact, a lot of people in town would be rid of him."

"He has other partners in town?"

"I wouldn't call them partners," she said. "In fact, I'm not sure *I'm* his partner. I feel more like his . . . captive. He has this attitude that he not only owns my businesses, he owns me."

"Have you ever given him any reason to think that?" he asked.

She stiffened a moment, then said, "No, not ever. He knows exactly what I think of him. I let him know every time he comes around."

"How's he feel about that?"

She looked frustrated. "It only seems to excite him," she admitted. "I try to keep my feelings to myself, but when he's around I can't help myself." She put her hand

on his arm again. "Between Cantrell and my husband,
I'd given up on men—until now."

"What's different now?"

She moved in on him and said, "You walked into my
store today."

Then she was in his arms and they were locked in a
molten-hot kiss.

TWENTY-EIGHT

Clint pulled her shirt out of her jeans, slid his hands underneath. Her flesh was smooth and hot. He pushed his other hand down the back of her pants, slid his middle finger along the crease between her buttocks. Her ass cheeks held his finger tightly.

She pulled his shirt free, ran her hands over his chest.

"It's been a long time for me," she said against his mouth. "I can't wait . . ."

"Where's the bedroom?" he asked.

"In the back."

She was a big woman. She probably weighed about 160, but he lifted her and carried her to the bedroom. He set her on the bed and started to undress. She pulled off her boots, shimmied out of her jeans, and hastily pulled her shirt over her head.

Her breasts were heavy; those faint freckles on her face were also across her chest, deep in her cleavage. Her nipples were russet colored, already hard.

When he was naked, she reached for his penis, stroked it until it was hard and long. She stared at it, then leaned forward and kissed it.

"I thought you couldn't wait," he said, "because now I can't."

"Feel me . . ." she said, spreading her legs.

He put his hand there, felt how hot and wet and slick she was.

"Yeah, you're ready . . ." he said, probing.

She caught her breath, held his dick, tight in her hand.

"So are you," she said, tugging on him. "Come, on, come on . . ."

He got onto the bed with her, knelt between her legs, and pressed his cock to her wet pussy. She gasped as he slid himself up and down, and then again when he pushed into her.

"Yesss," she said, drawing her knees up, "oh, yes . . ."

He took her in long, slow strokes, but she urged him to go faster.

"Come on," she said, "I told you it's been a long time. Make love to me later. Fuck me now!"

He did.

He slid his hands beneath her to grasp her ass, then fucked her hard, pulling her to him each time he drove into her.

Her eyes went wide and the cords on her neck stood out. She released her knees and wrapped her legs around him, locking them in.

"How long can you last?" she hissed into his ear.

"Longer than you," he said.

She laughed, then cried, and said, "Good!"

* * *

Hours later, they rolled apart, gasping.

"For someone . . . who hasn't been with a man . . . in a while . . . that was pretty good."

"Well," she said, putting her hand on his belly, "I was . . . always kind of . . . good at it. You're . . . no slouch . . . yourself."

He took her hand, held it tightly, his eyes closed.

"Don't go to sleep on me, Gunsmith," she said. "I'm not finished with you, yet."

"I'm not finished, either," he promised. "I just need to . . . catch my breath."

"Well," she said, "yeah, I could . . . do that, too."

They fell asleep.

They woke during the night and rolled toward each other. This time, they made love slowly. She rode him for a while, with him kissing and licking her breasts and nipples, and then they reversed. Later they spooned, and he slid his dick up between her thighs and into her. They moved slowly together, gently, then he withdrew and eased his penis—slick with her juices—into her anus.

"Oooh, damn," she said. "There's something nobody's done to me before."

"Sorry," he said, "I should have asked first."

He started to withdraw, but she said, "No," and clamped down on him. "I think I have the hang of this, already."

She moved again, and so did he.

"Oh yes, see?" she asked. "This is . . . very intimate."

"It's all intimate, Mrs. Mason," he said, hugging her tightly to him.

"Yes," she said, dreamily, "it is, isn't it, Mr. Adams?"

TWENTY-NINE

Clint stayed all night, and woke in the morning to the smell of bacon. He got dressed and went to the kitchen, found Lisa at the stove.

"Good morning," she said, over her shoulder. "Something else I haven't done with a man in a long time. I hope you don't mind."

"Not at all," he said. "I'm starving."

"Have a seat."

He sat at the table and she brought him a mug of coffee. He could tell from the smell it was just the way he liked it.

"You strike me as a strong coffee man."

"Exactly."

He sipped it while she watched him. "Perfect."

"Like the whole night," she said. She kissed him shortly and returned to the stove. "Yesterday morning, I had a cup of coffee here alone, never expecting what the day would bring."

"Some surprises are good, huh?" he asked.

"This one was," she said. "Generally speaking, I don't like surprises."

"Neither do I."

She came to the table with two plates of bacon and eggs. "I didn't have the makings for biscuits," she said apologetically.

"This looks great," he assured her.

While they ate, she told him that she planned to finish what she'd been doing in the Gun Shop but that she'd be available later if he wanted to get together.

"You know," she finished, "if you want to eat . . . or something."

He smiled at her and said, "I don't really have my day all planned out the way you do, Lisa, so we'll have to see."

"That's right," she said. "You're still going after Cantrell."

"Or whoever the killer is."

"Well," she said, going back to their conversation of the day before, "if the motive was profit, your killer has to be Harry Cantrell."

"My feelings exactly."

Cantrell rolled over in bed and looked at his wife. She was lying naked on her side, facing him. Her large breasts looked like partially deflated bags. There was a roll of fat around her midsection. He was always amazed how she could fill him with lust at night, and disgust him in the morning. But she'd had many men, so he knew it wasn't just him. She was just very, very good in bed.

Even though Cantrell had other women in town—a couple of whores, a waitress, and a business colleague's wife—and they were all more attractive than his wife, he always came back to her. He had to admit that none of them were as good as she was at sex. She had the talents of a top-notch whore.

He slid out of bed without waking her, slipped on a robe, and went downstairs to the kitchen. He didn't keep servants. He didn't trust anyone that much to allow them the run of his house.

He made coffee and sat at the table drinking it. He knew she'd be down in a few minutes. He didn't like the hold she had over him. Maybe he should take Eddie Pratt up on his offer to kill her.

He heard her coming down the stairs, poured her a cup of coffee.

"Good mornin', lover," she said.

After the coffee, she went to the stove to prepare breakfast. "We're going to have to get some servants," she said, with her back to him.

"No."

"At least a cook," she said calmly.

"I said no," Cantrell said. "I don't want strangers in the house."

"Well," she said, turning to face him, "once we had a cook here for several weeks she wouldn't be a stranger anymore, would she?"

"Damn it, Ava!" he snapped.

"Well," she said, turning back to the stove, "maybe the more you have to eat my cooking, the faster you'll agree."

It was true. She might have been good in bed, but in the kitchen Ava was a disaster.

Okay, so maybe just a cook.

THIRTY

Eddie Pratt rolled over, looked at the whore in bed with him . . .

He'd gone to the whorehouse the evening before, had all the whores gather in the sitting room, and then picked out the best-looking one.

"Get her to my hotel tonight," he told the madam. "She's gonna spend the night."

"Sure thing, cowboy," the madam said.

The whore went up to her room to get ready. Before he could leave, though, a cute little blonde, not his type at all, sidled up next to him and said, "The best lookin' ain't always the best."

"That right?" he asked.

She looked up at him from beneath impossibly long lashes and said. "Yep, it is."

He noticed something about her he hadn't noticed

from across the room. The way her hair smelled. And when she touched his arm . . .

"Still here?" the madam asked.

He turned to her and said, "This girl." He looked at the girl. "What's your name?"

"Annie."

"I want this one. Annie."

"But—"

"I changed my mind," he said. "This one."

The madam shrugged and said, "Suit yourself. Get ready, Annie."

"I'm ready now," Annie said, smiling at him. "Shall we go?"

He leaned over now and smelled her hair. It still had that heady scent to it, just like the hair between her legs. And the sun coming through the window made the down on her arms shine.

But even more than the smell of her was her talent. He had no doubt that she was the right choice. The other whore could not have been more talented than she was.

Pratt usually liked bigger women—tall, full-bodied. Annie was small, petite, with hardly any breasts, but she had a great butt, and her nipples were mesmerizing.

And there didn't seem to be anything she wouldn't do.

She opened her eyes slow, caught him looking at her.

"So?" she asked.

"So what?"

"Was I right?"

He reached out and touched her smooth thigh. "You were right," he said. "No doubt."

Her smile widened. She sat up in bed, put her hand on his bare thigh.

"You gonna be in town long?"

"I don't know," he said. "Long as it takes."

"You have a job?"

"I have a job I have to do," he said. "After that I might have to leave for a while."

"What kind of job?" she asked. "What do you do?"

He stared at her for as moment, then decided to try to shake her up.

"I kill people."

Her eyes widened. "Really? For money?"

"That's right."

"You've killed people already?"

"Uh-huh."

Rather than being shaken up, she looked excited. "How do you do it?"

"With my gun."

She reached out, took his right hand, and pulled it to her chest. She held it there so he could feel her smooth skin, and the heart beating beneath it.

"With this hand?"

"Yes."

She took hold of his index finger, lifted it to her mouth, sucked it in, then slid it out. It glistened wetly.

"With this finger?"

"My trigger finger," he said. "Yeah."

"Ooh," she said.

She brought his finger down to her chest, between her breasts, then down farther, over her belly, navel and down into the tangle of golden hair between her legs.

She opened her legs slightly and pressed his finger to her wet slit.

"This finger kills people?" she asked.

"Yes."

"Mmmm." She closed her eyes and slid his finer inside her steamy depth. When she released him he slid his finger in and out of her, causing her to catch her breath and bite her bottom lips.

"Are you ready to get out of bed?" she asked him.

"Not yet," he said, pushing her down onto her back. "Not yet!"

He took hold of her ankles, spread her, and rammed his hard dick into her.

THIRTY-ONE

"You ever heard of Eddie Pratt?" the sheriff asked Clint.

"No."

They were in the Three-Leaf Clover saloon. The sheriff had called to Clint on the street and invited him in, even though the place was not yet open. Only the sheriff, Clint, and the bartender were present.

"Who is he?" Clint asked.

"A money gun."

"I never heard of him."

"That's the way he likes it."

"No ego, then?" Clint asked. "That's unusual."

"You have an ego?"

"Of course," Clint said. "Most people with reputations have an ego. Some of us can keep it in check, though."

"Well, Pratt likes to do his job without attracting attention," Sheriff Glenister said.

"And does he work for Cantrell?"

"He works for anybody who will pay him," Glenister said. "That means he has worked for Cantrell."

"Anybody else in town who works for him?"

"There's a fella named Johnny Devlin around—which is kind of odd."

"Why?"

"Devlin usually works for Sutcliffe, in Roswell."

"So if he's here it's because Sutcliffe sent him. Was he here before me?"

"I think so."

"Sutcliffe sent him to warn Cantrell I was coming," Clint said. "And Cantrell sent for Pratt. Does Pratt work alone?"

"Sometimes," Glenister said, "but I don't think he's on his payroll."

"Where can I find Pratt?"

"He's stayin' in a hotel in the red-light district."

"You have a red-light district?"

"This town is growin'," Glenister said. "The place is called the Colorado."

"Why?" Clint asked.

Glenister just shrugged. "I think the guy who owns it is from Colorado," he said.

Clint put his half-empty beer mug down.

"Thanks for the drink."

"You gonna brace him?"

"I'm going to talk to him," Clint said. "That's what I've been doing, talking to everyone involved. By the way, where's Devlin staying?"

"Same place."

"That'll come in handy."

"You want my advice?"

"Sure."

"Talk to Devlin first."

"Why?"

"Because you can scare him," Glenister said. "You can get him to talk."

"Pratt doesn't scare?"

"Not that I know of."

"Well, I appreciate the advice," Clint said. "Like I said, I'm just going to talk to them."

"Yeah," Glenister said, dubiously, "that's your plan."

"Also," Clint said, "I want to check in Roswell to see if the family registered any property claims."

"You think Cantrell was after their property?"

"If killing them made him a profit, what else could it be?"

"If they came to Roswell with a deed and he killed them, don't you think he would have taken the deed? And erased any record of it?"

"I'm sure he would, but I'll have to check, anyway. I'll telegraph the sheriff there to do it for me."

"Do you trust him?"

"I'll have to," Clint said. "I don't want to have to ride back to Hondo and then back here again."

"Well, if you trust him," Sheriff Glenister said, "and he vouched for me, then I guess you trust me, too."

"Yes," Clint said, "I guess so."

Clint walked into the red-light district, not feeling any different. Usually the red-light district was a bad place to be, but this one looked the same as any other part of town.

He made his way toward the Colorado Hotel, a

two-story solid-looking structure. When he entered he woke the clerk, who came up off his hand and elbow with a start.

"What?"

"I just want to take a look at your register."

"You law?"

"No," Clint said, and grabbed the register. He turned the book around, opened it, saw that Eddie Pratt was in room four, and Johnny Devlin was in room seven.

"These rooms upstairs?" he asked.

"All the rooms are upstairs."

"Pratt and Devlin. You know them on sight?"

"Yeah," the clerk said warily. He was middle-aged, had a face filled with lines and crevices. He'd been through a lot in his life, and had given up a long time ago.

"They in their rooms?"

"Devlin is," the clerk said.

Clint closed the book and went upstairs. He came to room four and knocked, even though the clerk said Pratt was out. No harm checking. He put his ear to the door, knocked again, then moved on to room seven. This time when he knocked, it was answered right away.

"Johnny Devlin?"

Devlin took one look at him and his eyes widened. He staggered back a few steps, but didn't go for his gun.

"I didn't do nothin'," he said.

"I know it," Clint said. "I just want to talk to you. Can I come in?"

Devlin frowned. "You're askin' me?"

"It's your room, isn't it?"

"Well, yeah, but . . ."

"Can I come in?"

"S-sure."

Clint entered and swung the door closed behind him.

"You're nervous," Clint said.

"Well . . . you're the Gunsmith."

"How about you take your gun out of your leather and put it on the dresser. Just for now. So you don't do something silly."

"O-okay."

Devlin walked to the dresser, took the gun out, and set it down.

"Now move away from it."

Devlin did.

"Okay," Clint said. "Now we can talk."

THIRTY-TWO

"Whaddaya wanna talk about?" Devlin asked.

"You, Eddie Pratt, Harry Cantrell," Clint said. "Eleven dead people."

"I didn't have nothin' to do with that."

"Well, maybe not directly," Clint said. "But your boss did, didn't he?"

Devlin frowned, then asked, "M-Mr. Sutcliffe?"

"I'm talking about Cantrell."

"Mr. Sutcliffe is my boss."

"And he's partners with Mr. Cantrell."

For a moment Devlin looked as if he was going to cry. "Whaddaya want from me?"

"Just a little information," Clint said. "Where's Eddie Pratt?"

"W-who?"

"Come on, Johnny," Clint said. "I'm being nice here. I could be a lot less nice."

Devlin swallowed hard. "Pratt's got a room here," he said, "but I don't know where he is now. I swear."

"That's okay," Clint said. "I'll find him."

"Are—are you gonna kill him?"

"I don't know," Clint said. "I guess that'll have to be up to him."

"And me?"

"Same answer," Clint said. "It'll be up to you."

"I don't wanna die."

"Then there shouldn't be a problem."

"But I can't tell you anythin' else," Devlin said. "They don't talk to me, or tell me anything. I just . . . run errands."

"I see."

"I'm nobody important."

"Then I guess we're done here."

Clint turned and opened the door, then turned back. He saw Devlin looking over at his gun.

"Maybe you think killing me would make you important?" he asked.

"I wasn't—I wasn't thinkin'—"

"Yeah, you were," Clint said. "Like I said, don't give me a reason to kill you, Devlin."

"I-I won't."

"Good."

Clint left, closing the door behind him. He waited, giving Devlin time to grab his gun and come running out. When he didn't, Clint left.

When he got downstairs, he decided that rather than wander around town looking for Eddie Pratt, he'd be better served just sitting in front of the hotel and waiting.

He didn't know what the man looked like, but he had a feeling they'd know each other on sight.

It only took about an hour of sitting and watching people go by, before Eddie Pratt showed up. No one went in or out of the hotel during that time, but then a man came from across the street, and he knew it was Pratt. It was in the way he walked, carried himself, the way he reacted when he saw Clint sitting there.

"I wondered when you'd show up," Pratt said.

"Just thought we should talk."

"Sure. Let me get another chair."

Pratt went inside, came out with a chair, set it next to Clint's, and sat down.

"What's on your mind?"

"Your boss."

"What boss would that be?"

"Cantrell."

"Is he my boss?"

"Are we going to play games?"

Pratt shrugged. "It's all a game, ain't it?"

"Sometimes I think so," Clint said, "except when people die."

"You've killed your share."

"Never innocent people," Clint said. "You know your boss killed eleven people? Including children?"

"So you say."

"Or maybe," Clint suggested, "he had you do it?"

"Is this why you wanted to talk?" Pratt asked. "To try to get me to tell you something you need to know before you can make a move?"

"A move?"

"You can't move on Cantrell without proof," Pratt said. "Well, I'm not going to give it to you."

"Maybe," Clint said, "you just did."

Pratt looked at Clint. "I'm not about to step into the street with you," he said.

"Not even if Cantrell tells you to?"

Pratt laughed. "He can't pay me enough to commit suicide."

"You mean you're not like all the others?" Clint asked. "All the ones who wanted to test themselves against me? Wanted to prove they were faster? Make a name for themselves?"

"I have a name," Pratt said. "My own name. I don't need yours."

Clint's eyes locked on Pratt's, and he believed the man. He didn't see any ego there. Pratt might turn out to be one of his most dangerous foes yet.

He stood up. "I'm going to take down your boss, Pratt," he said. "He has to pay for what he did to those people. Don't get in my way."

"You'll need proof," Pratt said, again.

"Maybe not," Clint said.

"What's that mean?"

"I just have to satisfy myself that he had those people killed," Clint said. "Once I've done that, I'll take care of him—and whoever he used to do it—myself."

"You know, over the years your reputation has changed," Pratt said, "Last I heard, you weren't a cold-blooded killer."

"I'll do whatever I have to do to get justice for those people."

THIRTY-THREE

When Devlin opened his door to another knock, he hoped he wouldn't find Clint Adams standing there. Instead, he saw Eddie Pratt.

"Let's go," Pratt said.

"Where?" Devlin asked.

"We got things to do," Pratt said. "I just talked to Adams outside. He doesn't sound like he's gonna wait to get proof— Wait a minute."

Devlin averted his eyes.

"Was he here, too?" Pratt asked. "Did he talk to you?"

"Uh, yeah, he came here."

"And what did you tell him?"

"Nothin'!" Devlin said. "I didn't tell him nothin' because I don't know nothin'. I'm just an errand boy, Pratt."

Pratt looked around the room, saw Devlin's gun on the dresser.

"Leather your gun and let's go."

* * *

"Where are we goin'?" Devlin asked when they got to the street.

"To find two more men who are workin' with us," Pratt said.

"Workin' with us . . . to do what?"

"To do what we were hired to do."

"And what's that?"

"Kill the Gunsmith."

Devlin stopped walking. Pratt went a few steps before he realized it. He stopped, turned around, then walked back to stand next to Devlin.

"What?"

"I wasn't hired to kill anybody," Devlin said. "That's not what I do."

"What do you do, Johnny?"

"I run errands."

"For who?"

"For Mr. Sutcliffe and Mr. Cantrell."

"Well," Pratt said, "that's what this is. An errand for them."

"But . . . I ain't never killed nobody."

Pratt slapped him on the back. "There's a first time for everything."

They remained in the red-light district, went from saloon to whorehouse and back again until Pratt found the three men he'd hired—two of them were in a saloon, drinking together and arguing, while the third was in a fleabag whorehouse pounding away at a pimply two-dollar whore.

To the two guys in the saloon, Pratt said, "Stay here. We're gonna look for Sinclair and come back."

Davey and Danny Wilkes could have been brothers, but they were cousins, both in their late twenties.

"Okay," Davey said.

"And don't get drunk!" Pratt said.

"Okay," Danny said.

As soon as Pratt and Devlin left, the cousins ordered a bottle of whiskey.

At the whorehouse, Pratt asked for Sinclair and was told he was with Simone.

"What room?" he asked.

"Um, five, but he ain't do—"

"Maybe," Pratt said to Devlin, "we can get to him before his dick falls off from some disease."

"Hey—" the madam said, but they brushed past her and went upstairs.

When they got to room five, Pratt slammed the door open so hard that Sinclair jumped off the whore he was fucking. He was tall, very thin, and had a huge penis. The whore was also long and skinny . . . and ugly. It was hard to tell her pimples from her breasts.

"Jesus, man—" Sinclair said.

"Get dressed!" Pratt said. "If you want to get paid."

"Can't I finish here?"

"No," Pratt said. "We probably saved you from gettin' a disease. We'll wait downstairs." Pratt took a look at the skinny whore. She had a wide, thin-lipped mouth and long, stringy black hair and seemed to be in her forties. "If you paid two dollars, you're gettin' gypped."

Pratt and Devlin left, with Devlin feeling sick, either from seeing the ugly whore, or Sinclair's huge dick.

After they were gone, Sinclair looked down at his raging erection.

"Simone, over here, quick!"

"But—"

"Hurry."

The skinny whore got off the bed and went over to him. He forced her to her knees and said, "Open your mouth!"

"But—"

"If you wanna get paid!" he shouted.

She opened her mouth.

THIRTY-FOUR

After sending a telegram to Hondo, Clint went to the Three-Leaf Clover saloon for a cold beer. It was midday, so there were only a few other men there, lingering over drinks. Clint chose to stand at the bar.

His telegram had asked Sheriff Scott in Hondo to check and see if anyone in the dead Eckert family had filed a deed for property in the Hondo area. He then checked in Carrizozo and found that there had been no deed filed by them.

He lingered over his beer, wondering what he could do next. He had no proof, no evidence that Harry Cantrell had poisoned the Eckert family, or had them poisoned, but he felt sure he had done it. But sure enough to take the law into his own hands?

Probably not.

Unless somebody had forced the issue.

Maybe all he had to do was wait for Cantrell to send Pratt after him.

* * *

Pratt told Devlin to take Sinclair back to the saloon where they'd left the Wilkes brothers.

"I'm gonna talk to Cantrell and then meet you all over there."

"Okay."

"Don't let them get drunk!" Pratt said. "We might have to do this today."

"Yeah, okay."

They split up, and Pratt headed for Cantrell's office.

Pratt walked into Cantrell's office while the businessman was talking to two men. His boss gave him a warning shake of the head. Pratt went and looked out the window until Cantrell had completed his business.

"I'll get right back to you with the final numbers," Cantrell said, as he walked the two men to the door, "but I think we're going to be able to do business."

After he ushered the two businessmen out the door, he locked it and turned to Pratt.

"Is it done?" he asked.

"You said you didn't want it done too soon," Pratt said, "but I thought you ought to know . . ."

"You think he'd do it?" Cantrell asked after Pratt had related his conversation with Clint Adams.

"Kill you?"

"Of course kill me, what else are we talkin' about?" Cantrell demanded.

"Sure, he could do it," Pratt said.

"But will he?"

"If he can't find the proof he wants," Pratt said, "I think he might."

"Then you have to do it," Cantrell said, "and soon."

"You don't want to talk to the sheriff first?" Pratt asked.

"The sheriff in this town is somethin' I don't own," Cantrell said. "The badge actually means somethin' to the fat bastard."

"Well," Pratt said, "if I have to go up against the law and Clint Adams . . ."

"What?" Cantrell asked. "More money?"

"Well . . ."

"Damn it, Pratt!" Cantrell said. "How about this? If you actually have to kill the sheriff, I'll pay you extra. How's that?"

Pratt sat back in his chair and said, "That'll work."

"Now," Cantrell said, "on another matter, remember what we were talking about last time . . . about my wife . . . ?"

THIRTY-FIVE

Clint decided that instead of waiting for Cantrell to send Pratt after him, he'd force the businessman's hand.

He went from the saloon to the sheriff's office. Glenister wasn't there, so he started to walk toward Cantrell's office. On the way, though, he ran into Glenister.

"Small town," he said. "We keep running into each other."

"I try to keep an eye on everythin'," the lawman said.

"I haven't seen any of your deputies while I've been here," Clint said.

"They're around," Glenister said. "I tell my boys to keep a low profile. Where are you off to now?"

"To see Cantrell."

"Gonna push 'im?"

"I thought I'd try a shove," Clint said.

"Get him to come after you?"

"Get him to send Pratt after me," Clint said. "Had a talk with Pratt."

"How'd that go?"

"We understand each other."

"Is that good?" the lawman asked.

"We'll see."

"Want me to come with you?"

"How would you justify that?" Clint asked.

Glenister shrugged. "Just tryin' to keep the peace."

Clint gave it a moment's thought, then said, "Why not? Let's see what happens."

As Clint and the sheriff entered Cantrell's office, the man looked up from his desk and frowned. He opened his top drawer.

"If you've got a gun in that drawer you're being a little premature, Cantrell."

The man froze.

"Besides," Clint added, "you'd have to shoot the sheriff, too."

"I wouldn't like that, Mr. Cantrell," Glenister said.

"What the hell are you two doing here?" Cantrell demanded. He closed the door slowly. "Sheriff, what are you doing with this man?"

"I'm just here to make sure he don't shoot you," the sheriff said.

"Or you me," Clint said.

"Have your say, Adams, and get out," Cantrell said. "I'm a businessman, and I don't have time to waste with the likes of you."

"I just wanted you to know I talked to your boys," Clint said.

"What boys is that?"

"Devlin and Pratt."

"Devlin works for my partner Sutcliffe," Cantrell said. "Pratt I employ from time to time."

"This being one of those times," Clint said.

"Do you purport to know all of my employees now, Adams?"

"Not all," Clint said. "Just the one who have been hired to kill me."

"And why would I want to kill you?"

"Because I've got you figured out, Cantrell," Clint said. "I know why you had the Eckert family killed."

"Is that the family you say was poisoned?"

"That's them."

"Wouldn't I have come up with an easier way to kill them?" the businessman asked. "Why poison?"

"I don't know, but that's one of the things I'm going to find out."

THIRTY-SIX

Clint and the sheriff left Cantrell's office, with the lawman shaking his head.

"If he could've killed you with a look, you'd be dead," Glenister said.

"You think he'll come after me?"

"Somebody will," the sheriff said. "Probably Pratt."

"On Cantrell's payroll."

"If you can avoid killing Pratt, and then get him to admit he was on Cantrell's payroll, then we'd have something."

"It's not always possible to not kill someone who's trying to kill you," Clint said.

"I'm sure," Glenister said. "You'll just have to do what you have to do."

"Well," Clint said, "when he does, I don't think Pratt will come alone. His job is to kill me, not to kill me in a fair fight."

"Well," the sheriff said, "when I hear the shots I'll come a-runnin'."

"Appreciate that, Sheriff," Clint said, "but when it happens it'll probably happen fast."

After Clint Adams and Sheriff Glenister left, Cantrell opened his top drawer and took out the gun. He was tempted to run to the door, slam it open, and shoot both of them in the back. He squeezed the gun tightly, not knowing what to do with the urge to shoot somebody.

He'd already given Pratt the okay to go after Clint Adams. There was no reason for him to look for the man again, or even to be in town when it happened.

He stood up, tucked the gun into his belt, then buttoned his jacket and left the office.

Pratt gathered his men at the red-light district saloon. The Wilkeses were still working on their bottle of whiskey.

"I thought I told you not to let them get drunk," he said to Devlin.

"They were drunk when I got here," Devlin said. "How am I supposed to take the bottle away from them? They'd kill me!"

Sinclair, who was still upset about being pulled away from his pimply whore, walked to the table where the Wilkes cousins were sitting, grabbed the whiskey bottle, and smashed it on the table. Glass and rotgut flew everywhere.

"No more drinkin'!" he shouted.

The two cousins stared up at him.

"Okay," Davey said.

"Sure," Danny said.

Sinclair turned to Pratt and spread his arms.

"I'm gettin' a beer," he said.

"Okay," Pratt said, when Sinclair returned with his mug, "today's the day we take Adams."

"It's gettin' late," Sinclair said.

"Yeah, we're gonna do it after dark."

"How?" Davey asked.

"We're gonna ambush him."

"In the dark?" Danny asked.

"On the street?" Sinclair asked.

"Yeah."

"That ain't gonna do nothin' for your reputation," Davey said to Pratt.

"Maybe not," Pratt said, "but it's gonna be great for my wallet."

THIRTY-SEVEN

Clint found Lisa at the mercantile.

"Finish at the Gun Shop?" he asked.

"Yep," she said, "I'm just finishing some stuff up here. Can we . . . take up where we left off?"

"I don't think so, Lisa."

"Why not?" she asked. "Look, if you're afraid I'm going to get too attached to you, don't worry. I'm a big girl."

"Yeah," he said, "that's why I know I can tell you. It's not safe."

"Not safe?"

"Are we alone?"

"Yes, I sent the clerk home. We can put the CLOSED sign up and—"

"Let me explain," he said. He tried.

"So," she said, "you're telling me that you expect somebody to try to kill you in the next few hours?"

"Yes," he said.

"And this is something you set up?"

"Yes, it is," he said. "And it's not safe for you to be around."

"And how safe is it for you?"

"Not safe at all," he said, "but that's kind of the point."

"Can I ask questions?"

"Sure."

"Is this the only way you think of to get this done?"

"Yes."

"Is Cantrell going to come after you himself?"

"Oh, no," Clint said. "He'll send somebody."

"How many somebodies?"

"I don't know," Clint said. "Two that I know of, maybe more. Four. Five."

"And do you have any help?"

"Um, the sheriff said he'll come running when he hears shots."

"That could mean that by the time he gets there, you're dead."

"That's possible."

She looked at him as if he was crazy.

"And you're good enough with that gun of yours that facing five men doesn't worry you?"

"Well, yes . . . I mean, yeah I'm good with a gun, and yeah it worries me, but . . ."

"But what?"

"But this is what I do, Lisa," Clint said. "And since I'm expecting them, I should be in control."

"Control?" she asked. "One against five?"

"Don't worry about it—"

"Look," she said, "I own a gun shop, and I'm pretty good with a gun. I could—"

"No!"

"Just to back you up—"

"I said no," he said. "Having to worry about you would definitely get me killed. And you!"

"It was just a thought."

"Well, it was a bad one. Just put it out of your mind."

"Okay."

"Hopefully, this should all be over by this time tomorrow," he said.

"Have you gotten word about whether or not it really was poison?"

"No," Clint said, "I'm sure the doc in Hondo is still waiting for word from Sante Fe."

"That's the part that really puzzles me," Lisa said. "Why poison them? Why not just shoot them all and be done with it?"

"Maybe he was hoping people would think they died of a disease," Clint said. "Then nobody would be looking for a killer."

"Except you."

"Except me."

"Guess he was pretty unlucky that you're the one who found the bodies. Anyone else would probably have just run at the sight of them."

"It's sad," he said, "but you're probably right about that. I better get going. They can't try to kill me if they can't find me."

She walked him to the door.

"Stay inside," he said. "And if you hear shooting, don't come out until it's all over. Understand?"

"Of course I understand," she said. "Don't come out until you're dead."

She took his face in her hands and kissed him tenderly. "Please be careful."

"Careful," he said, "is my middle name."

No, she thought as he walked out, *stubborn* is!

THIRTY-EIGHT

Harry Cantrell entered his house and stopped in the entry foyer. The gun was heavy in his belt. He listened, couldn't hear anything. Either Ava wasn't home, or for a change she was being quiet.

Then he heard it: familiar sounds. A man and a woman together. Coming from upstairs.

He went up, walking quietly along the hall. The sounds—moans, flesh-on-flesh slaps—got louder as he got closer to the bedroom.

When he got to the door he peered around. There was Ava, naked on the bed, on all fours, a man fucking her from behind.

"Come on," she said, "harder, damn it."

"I'll give it to you harder, bitch," the man grunted.

Ava's black hair was stringy with sweat, her body covered with a sheen of perspiration. The room was filled with the smell of her. Cantrell felt himself growing hard.

He took the gun from his belt, cocked the hammer, and stepped into the room.

When Clint got to the street, his back started to itch. He had nobody in town he could count on to watch his back, so he was going to have to be extra alert.

He walked to his hotel, got a chair from inside, brought it out with him, and sat down. It was still a few hours until dark. If he was Eddie Pratt, he'd wait for darkness to fall and then execute an ambush. Since there was no question of Pratt facing him man to man, that seemed to be the best bet.

Sitting with his back to the hotel's wall, there wasn't much chance of an ambush. At least not from behind. But once it got dark, he'd stand up and give Pratt a chance to take his best shot. He'd probably have Johnny Devlin with him, and a few other men. Devlin wasn't somebody he was going to have to worry about, and the others would probably be cheap gun talent. Pratt was the one he was going to have to watch.

For now, though, he'd sit back and relax for a while.

"Did you see him?" Pratt asked.

Devlin sat opposite Pratt. The others were standing at the bar.

"He's sittin' in front of his hotel."

"Sittin'?"

"Just sittin'."

Pratt frowned.

"We gotta get him to move."

"He's gotta eat," Devlin suggested.

"Yeah, but he may just go into the hotel and eat there," Pratt said. "We need him on the street."

"How do we get 'im there?"

Pratt thought for a moment, then said, "We send him a message. Get him to meet somebody somewhere. Only when he gets there . . ."

". . . it's us."

"Right."

"Who do we send him a message from?"

"That's your job."

"What?"

"You been in town longer than I have," Pratt said. "Find out who he's made friends with, or who he's had dealings with."

"How am I supposed to do that?"

"Ask."

"Harry!" Ava said, when she saw him.

"What?" the man on the bed said. Then he saw the gun. "Hey!"

He withdrew from Ava and jumped off the bed, his dick waving around in front of him.

"Harry, damn it, you're ruining it!" Ava said, turning and sitting on her butt.

"Where'd you get this one?" Cantrell asked.

"He came riding in asking for water," she said.

"And you gave him more than water."

She smiled, gnawed on a nail. He noticed how hard her nipples looked.

Then he looked at the man. Young, well built, not particularly well endowed but he seemed to be doing the job.

"She's not much to look at, is she?" he asked.

The young man didn't answer. He tried to hide his cock and balls, looking frightened.

"But she's good in bed, right?"

"Look, Mister," the man said, "I didn't know she was married—"

"Yeah, you did," Cantrell said. "She always tells them she's married."

"Them?"

"You don't think you're the first, do you?"

"Mister," the man said, "I just earnin' my meal—"

"Yeah," Cantrell said, "I know."

Cantrell fired. The bullet hit the man in the chest. His arms got flung wide and then Cantrell shot him in the groin.

"Harry," Ava said, "I'm impressed. You've never shot one before. Jealous?"

"Shut up, bitch" Cantrell said.

He put the gun aside, dropped his own trousers, revealing his erect penis.

Ava got on all fours, hiked her butt up into the air, and said, "Come to Momma, baby."

Cantrell removed the rest of his clothes and got on the bed with his sweaty wife. He slapped her on the ass hard enough to leave a red handprint.

"Ow! Harry, oh yes."

He grabbed her hips, ignored the sweaty sheets beneath them and drove himself into her from behind.

THIRTY-NINE

Clint Adams was a man people noticed. Johnny Devlin went around town asking questions, like Pratt had told him, and came back with the answers.

"What've you got?" Pratt asked.

"Adams has only been seen with two people. One is Sheriff Glenister."

"And the other one?"

"A woman," Devlin said. "Her name is Lisa Mason. She owns a couple of businesses in town. The mercantile and the Gun Shop."

"Gun Shop?"

"That's right."

"Wait a minute," Pratt said, "doesn't Cantrell have a piece of that?"

Devlin nodded and said, "And the mercantile."

"So this Mason woman is his partner?"

"I guess so."

"He doesn't like having partners, does he?" Pratt asked.

"No," Devlin said, "he's always tryin' to get rid of them."

"Okay," Pratt said, "we'll use the Mason woman to get Adams out in the open."

"How?" Devlin asked.

"You're gonna deliver a message."

"A note?" Devlin asked. "What if he knows it's not her handwriting."

"Then it won't be a note," Pratt said. "You'll just tell him."

"Tell him what?"

Pratt drank some beer, licked his lips, and said, "I'm still thinkin' on that part."

It wasn't dark yet when the telegraph operator came walking over.

"Mr. Adams?"

"That's right."

"This came for you, sir," the clerk said. "It was marked rush."

"Thanks."

Clint unfolded the telegram, read it, then got up from his chair, and headed for the sheriff's office.

When Devlin got to Clint's hotel he saw that the chair in front was empty.

"Damn it," he said. "Now what?"

He turned and headed back to the red-light district.

Clint entered the sheriff's office and caught the man apparently meeting with his deputies.

"Lonny and Jim," Glenister said, "My deputies."

Clint nodded. The two young lawmen stared at him in awe.

"Just got this," Clint said, handing Glenister the telegram.

The lawman read it, then looked at Clint and said, "So they were poisoned."

"They don't know what it was," Clint said, "but yeah, there was something. They must have had somebody rush the samples to Santa Fe."

Glenister handed the telegram back. "If we knew what the poison was we could check if any of Cantrell's businesses used it, or carried it."

"We still don't have any evidence," Clint said.

"So you're still gonna wait for him to send somebody after you?" Deputy Lonny asked.

"That's right," Clint said. "That's all I can think to do."

"What if they actually kill you?" the other deputy, Jim, asked.

"Well then, hopefully you'll be able to arrest somebody and get them to turn on Cantrell."

"You boys get out there," Glenister said.

"You keeping them away from the hotel?" Clint asked.

"They'll just be makin' their rounds," the sheriff said. "At the sound of any shootin', we'll be there."

"Appreciate it, Sheriff," Clint said. "If they see any badges around they may not try."

The two young deputies put on their hats and left the office.

"They wanna back you," Glenister said.

"I appreciate it, but I hope they'll listen and stay away."

"You figure they'll come for you at the hotel?"

"No," Clint said, "I think they'll try to draw me away, somehow."

"How?"

"Maybe a message from you."

"You get a message from me, you'll know it's a phony," Glenister said.

"There's only one other person in town who might send me a message," Clint said. "One that I'd respond to, I mean."

"Cantrell?" Glenister asked.

"No, Lisa Mason."

"One of Cantrell's partners?"

"Reluctant partner."

"He's got lots of those," Glenister said.

"I'm going to head back to the hotel," Clint said. "Might go inside for a bite to eat, then I'll be back in the chair."

"Me and my boys'll be ready."

"Why are you going along with me on this, Sheriff?" Clint asked. "A lot of lawmen wouldn't stand for it."

"Cantrell's been runnin' roughshod over this county for long enough," Glenister said. "And if he killed those people, I want him to go down for it."

"Can't blame you for that," Clint said. "I'll see you when it's over."

"I hope so," Glenister said.

FORTY

Pratt watched as Devlin reentered the saloon and approached his table.

"Now what?"

"He ain't there."

"Well, where is he?"

"I dunno."

"Well, find him, Johnny," Pratt said.

"And deliver the same message?"

"What else?"

"I dunno—"

"Yes, deliver the same message!"

"Okay."

As Devlin went back outside, Pratt muttered, "Idiot."

At another table, Sinclair was watching the Wilkes cousins work their way slowly through a mug of beer each. No more whiskey for them.

* * *

Cantrell rolled off his wife onto his back, trying to catch his breath.

"Jesus, Harry," Ava said. "What got into you tonight?"

"Stress," he said.

"You should feel stress every night," she said, reaching down to rub between her legs. "You fucked me sore and raw."

He turned his head, looked at the dead man on the floor. Ava was lucky she had a lover with her, because he had to kill something tonight.

"And you killed a man!" she said.

"I know."

She sat up and took a look. "Yep, he's dead. How do we get him out of here?"

"I'll have a couple of boys take him out."

"What are you gonna tell them?"

"That he broke in and attacked you, and I shot him," Cantrell said.

She fell onto her back again, making her floppy tits jiggle. "You've got a story for everything, don't you?" she asked.

"Yes," he said, "I do."

After having some supper in the hotel dining room, Clint came back out to his chair and sat down. It was only a few minutes later when Johnny Devlin came walking along, looking surprised to see him there.

"Been lookin' for you," Devlin said.

"I've been here."

"I was here before, you wasn't."

"Well," Clint said, "I had to go inside to get something to eat. What's on your mind?"

"I got a message for you."

"From who?"

"Mrs. Mason."

"What's she want?"

"Says she wants you to meet her at Mr. Cantrell's office at nine o'clock."

"Tonight?"

"Well, yeah . . ."

"Kind of late, isn't it?"

Devlin nodded. "She said she had some business with him, and she wants your help."

"Why would she give you the message?"

He shrugged again. "Because that's what I do," he said. "I'm everybody's errand boy."

Devlin seemed honestly bitter about it.

"Okay, Devlin," Clint said. "You delivered your message. Now I have some advice for you."

"What advice?"

"Don't be there."

"What?"

"Don't be there at nine o'clock. You don't want to catch any flying lead."

"What? Lead?"

"That's right."

Devlin stared at Clint. He figured the man was either wondering what the hell he was talking about, or was wondering how he knew he was being set up.

"Just go, Devlin," Clint said. "Go away."

Devlin, still looking confused, went.

And when he entered the saloon to tell Pratt that he'd delivered the message, he was still confused. Should he tell Pratt that Adams seemed to know that he was being lured into a trap?

"Well, you idiot?" Pratt asked. "Did you deliver the message?"

"Yeah," Devlin said. "I delivered it."

"Then get yourself a beer."

Let's see, Devlin thought as he walked to the bar, who's going to be the idiot at nine o'clock?

FORTY-ONE

Clint checked the time, and at eight-forty-five he got up from his chair. He'd already checked both his guns—his Colt and his New Line—and both were in perfect working order. The New Line was tucked into the back of his belt.

The street was empty, and he considered that they might have been setting him up to be shot in the street on the way to his "meeting" with Lisa Mason. So he kept to the shadows as much as he could while making his way to Cantrell's office.

Within sight of the office he changed direction, ducked down at alley, and worked his way around to the back of the building. He hoped for Devlin's sake the man had taken his advice.

Pratt asked, "Where the hell is Devlin?"

"I dunno," Sinclair said.

"Idiot," Pratt said. "Where are the Wilkes brothers?"

"They're cousin—"

"Whatever!" Pratt said. "Where are they?"

"They're in position."

"Good. The four of us will do this without Devlin."

"He woulda got in the way, anyway," Sinclair said.

"That's kinda what I was countin' on," Pratt said.

Cantrell sat at the kitchen table while Ava made coffee. She was wearing a robe, but was naked under it. It swung open as she moved about, revealing sagging breasts and a bushy pubic patch. Cantrell didn't get it. What was it about her made men fall into bed with her? Maybe it was the way she smelled? Sweat, perfume, and sex. Right at that moment, he wanted to toss her on the table and fuck her again.

To distract himself, he thought about Pratt, Devlin, and whoever else Pratt had enlisted. Were they killing Clint Adams right at that moment? He hoped so. He didn't need the Gunsmith getting any deeper into his business.

Gradually, the smell of coffee began to overpower the scent of Ava.

"Here you go, Harry," she said, putting a cup in front of him. "Strong coffee for my big strong man." She cupped his chin, tilted his head up, and kissed him wetly. To his annoyance, it made his dick twitch.

"Ava," he said as she sat across from him, "if anyone asks, I was here all evening, and all night. Understand?"

"No," she said, "but that's okay. You're my husband and I'll lie for you. What about the two who carried the dead man out of here?"

"Don't worry," he said. "I'll go to the sheriff in the morning and tell him what happened."

"When are you going to replace that fat bastard?" she asked.

"As soon as I take control of the whole town," he said. "And the county."

"Well, replace him with somebody younger," she said. She reached into her robe to rub one of her nipples. "And somebody better looking."

Seeing her massage her own breasts and nipples started to get him worked up again.

"Ava, you're such a slut," he said.

"And you love it, don't you, Harry?"

Cantrell reached into her robe and grabbed one of her breasts, twisting cruelly.

"I love it as much as you do, you hot bitch," he told her. "Maybe we both love it too damn much."

She smiled at him, then frowned as he twisted even more and the pain became worse.

FORTY-TWO

Clint saw the man covering the back door. He didn't look particularly alert. In fact, he was working on his left thumbnail very earnestly with his teeth.

Clint was able to move up behind him very easily and press the barrel of his gun to the back of the man's neck.

"Just stand easy," Clint said, as the man stiffened. "Don't make a sound."

The man stood still.

Clint took the gun from the man's holster, reversed it, and brought the barrel down on the back of the man's head. It was something he never would have done with his own gun.

He caught the man as he fell and eased him to the ground. The man was wearing a neckerchief, so Clint removed it and used it to tie his victim's hands behind his back. It was just a safety measure. He figured the man would be unconscious long enough for Clint to get his work done.

That done, he tossed the man's gun into the darkness, then worked his way around to the front of the building. There he found another man. This one seemed a bit more alert, but he was staring off down the street and not paying attention to what might be coming from behind him.

This time, he pressed the barrel of his gun into the man's spine, grabbed him around the neck, and dragged him into the alley. Once again, he disarmed the man, used his own gun to knock him unconscious, and tied him up with his own neckerchief.

Two down. He figured Pratt was inside either alone, or with one other man—maybe Devlin, maybe not.

The question was, go in or call Pratt out? And if he went in, front door or back? Or a window?

If he had somebody with him, he'd have them toss a rock through a window. Then he'd bust in the back door. Of course, he could throw a rock through one window and then dive through the next one over, but with all that glass flying, he could end up getting hurt unnecessarily.

He moved to a window and peered inside. It was very dark and he couldn't see a thing inside. He waited a while, hoping his eyes would adjust, but he still saw nothing. Then, suddenly, he thought he saw a silhouette . . .

"Get down!" Pratt hissed as Sinclair suddenly stood up.

"My legs are fallin' asleep."

"Shut up!"

Pratt could have shot him.

Clint thought he heard voices, so he figured there were two men inside. There was no chance that one of them was Cantrell. He wouldn't risk his own life. It was more likely he was home in bed with his wife.

He could kick in a dolor—front or back—and simply fire at anything that moved. The moon was out and he'd be backlit if he tried that.

There was another way to go, but he'd be risking the life of one of the men he'd already taken out of play. Then again, they were all lying in wait to kill him, so . . .

He went around back, smacked the unconscious man awake, and then stood him up.

"Let's see how good your buddies inside are at telling us apart," he said.

"H-hey, Mister—"

"How any inside?"

"T-two."

"And the one in front makes four of you?"

"Y-yeah. That's my cousin."

"Uh-huh."

"Mister, ya—ya can't let them shoot me. T-that'd be murder."

"You were waiting to murder me."

"Yeah, but . . . we was gettin' paid!"

"Yeah," Clint said, "that explains it. Come on." He pushed the man toward the back door. "You yell before I open the door and I'll kill you myself. At least this way you've got a chance to survive. As soon as I open the door, you can yell your heart out, duck, whatever you want."

"Y-yeah, okay."

Clint walked him to the back door, pressed his gun against the man's lower back.

"Get ready," he whispered.

He lashed out with his right foot, driving his heel into the door just beneath the doorknob. Wood splintered, the door slammed open, and he pushed the man through the doorway.

"No, wait, wait!" the man started to yell. "It's me!"

The first two shots lit up the room, showing Clint where the shooters were. He waited for the third and fourth shots, and followed each of those with one of his own.

And then it was quiet.

FORTY-THREE

As promised, the sheriff and his deputies came running at the sound of shots. What they found were two dead men—Pratt and Sinclair—one wounded—Davey Wilkes—and one man who had come through unscathed—Danny Wilkes—except for a bump on his head.

Clint had lighted a lamp in the office and made the Wilkes boys sit together, with their hands tied behind them. Davey had taken a bullet in the shoulder, but Clint figured he'd live.

When the sheriff arrived, he left his deputies outside. He checked the two dead men when he came in.

"Dead center, once each," he said.

"He used me as a shield!" Davey complained.

"Shut up," Clint said. "You were here to kill me—you and your cousin."

"That true?" Glenister asked the wounded man.

Davey didn't answer until Clint nudged him from behind—in the injured shoulder.

"Ow! Yeah, I guess so."

"Who hired you?"

"Pratt."

"And who was he workin' for?" Glenister asked.

"I dunno."

Clint nudged him again.

"Ow! He never told us!"

"He's tellin' the truth," Danny said.

Glenister looked at Clint.

"Looks like you left the wrong two alive."

"There's still Devlin," Clint said. "He's out there, some-where."

"What about Cantrell?" Clint asked.

"What about him?"

"When he finds out what happened here, maybe he'll talk."

"When he comes in tomorrow and find a mess here?" the sheriff asked.

"I was thinking of riding out there tonight and telling him."

"Catch him off guard, huh?"

Clint nodded.

"Well, let me get these two in a cell and we'll mount up."

"My cousin needs a doctor," Danny complained.

"Yeah, he'll get one at the jail," Glenister said. "Come on, you two. Let's go."

Clint walked over to the jail with them, had some coffee while Glenister and one of his deputies locked the cousins up. The other deputy went for the doctor.

After that, they left the deputies at the office and went to the stable to saddle their horses.

Glenister groaned loudly as he climbed into the saddle. Clint thought it should have been his mare who did the groaning.

"You got that telegram with you? About the poison?" he asked Clint.

"Oh, yeah," Clint said, touching his pocket.

"How do you think Cantrell will react?"

"Maybe by surprising him we can get an honest reaction out of him . . . for a change."

They rode out of the livery and headed out of town.

"You know the way, right?" Clint asked. "It's pretty dark, even with the moon."

"Don't worry," Glenister said. "Most of the way will be on the main road."

They rode out side by side, both hoping tonight would bring the whole matter to an end. Glenister wanted the town—the whole county—to be rid of Harry Cantrell. Clint just wanted to finally find justice for those poor dead families.

FORTY-FOUR

When Clint and Glenister rode up to the house on the Cantrell ranch, they noticed something going on in the barn.

"What's that?" the lawman asked.

"Want to take a look?"

"Why not?"

They redirected their horses and rode over to the barn. They dismounted, walked to the barn door. There was a lot of light inside, and a circle of ranch hands standing around something.

"What's goin' on, boy?" Glenister asked.

They all turned to look, saw the light reflecting off the sheriff's badge. Clint stood to the sheriff's left, ready to back any play.

The men all looked confused, but backed away so the sheriff could see what they were looking at.

"Boys," the lawman said, "that looks an awful lot like a dead body."

Nobody spoke.

"Looks like a dead body to me," Clint said.

It was a man, lying on his back in the dirt, his chest and crotch bloody.

"You boys wanna tell me what happened here?" Glenister asked.

Once they had the story, Glenister warned the men not to move the body. In fact, he assigned two men to stand watch over it. One of them was the foreman, Andy Parker.

"Look, Sheriff," he said, "the boss said this guy broke into the house—"

"Just stay here, Andy," Glenister said. "And don't let anybody move this body. We'll go and talk to your boss."

"Okay," Parker said to the men, "you heard the sheriff. Everybody out."

Clint and the sheriff left with the other men, walked their horses over to the house.

"What do you think happened here?" Glenister asked Clint.

"From the stories I've heard about Cantrell's wife?" Clint said. "It could be true, but it still gives us something to pressure him with."

"True." Glenister nodded. "Still, it's unusual for Cantrell to do his own gunplay, in any situation."

"Maybe Mrs. Cantrell shot the man."

"Did you notice what I noticed about him?" the lawman asked.

"You mean the fact that he was naked?"

Glenister nodded.

"Whatever Mrs. Cantrell was doin' with him, I don't think she shot him."

They walked up the front steps of the house, tried the front door and, finding it locked, decided to knock. In the end, Glenister ended up pounding on it before it opened. Cantrell glared at them. His hair was a mess, and he was wearing a blue robe.

Harry Cantrell looked out at them and asked, "What the hell are you doing here?"

Clint was pleased to think he saw a look of disappointment on the man's face.

"Pratt's dead, Cantrell," Clint said. "And the Wilkes cousins gave you up."

"Who? What are you talking about, Adams?"

"We need to come in, Mr. Cantrell," Glenister said.

"I'll have your job for harassing me, Sheriff."

"Yeah, you can have it, if you want it," Glenister said, "but we're comin' in."

The lawman moved his bulk forward and Cantrell had to move or be bowled over. Clint followed.

"I demand to know why you're here," Cantrell said.

"We got the word from Santa Fe on the poison, Cantrell," the sheriff said.

"That again?"

"Somebody put poison in those people's food," Glenister said.

"Why would I do that?"

"Because they showed up with a deed to land you wanted, Cantrell," Clint said. "And they probably wouldn't sell, because it was going to be their home."

"And where would I get pois—"

"Come on," Clint said. "You own a ranch. You really think we won't find some poison out here, maybe used to get rid of critters?"

"And you probably own a couple of other businesses where poison is on the premises," Glenister said.

"You have no proof," Cantrell said, "no proof at all."

"We told you," Clint said, "the Wilkes cousins—"

"I have no idea who those people are."

"Eddie Pratt, a man named Sinclair, and the Wilkes cousins were waitin' to bushwhack Adams at your office."

"If somebody broke into my office, that's not my fault," Cantrell said.

Clint was disappointed. Cantrell was holding fast. Time to try another tact.

"Where's your wife, Cantrell?" Clint asked. "We'd like to ask her a few questions."

"My wife?" Cantrell asked. "She's, uh, sleeping."

"Would you like to explain to us," Glenister said, "why there's a dead man in your barn?"

"A naked dead man," Clint pointed out.

Clint thought he saw a muscle jump in Cantrell's jaw. He also saw something on the sleeve of Cantrell's robe. It looked a lot like blood.

"What?"

"Your men say you shot him when you found him in your house," Glenister said.

"Oh, that's, uh, that's right. He broke in."

"What was he doin' naked?" the sheriff asked.

"I don't know," Cantrell said. "Maybe he was crazy."

"If he was naked, he didn't have a gun," Glenister said. "So why did you shoot him?"

"He was attacking my wife," Cantrell said. "I'm afraid I didn't think. I just grabbed my gun and shot him."

"All the more reason we should talk to your wife," Clint said.

"I told you—"

"I smell coffee," Clint said. "You smell coffee, Sheriff?"

"Come to think of it," the lawman said, "I do."

"I made some," Cantrell said.

"Let's have a look in the kitchen," Clint suggested.

"No!" Cantrell said. "Uh, look . . ." He ran his hand through his hair. "Let me get dressed and I'll go out to the barn with you—"

"You can do that," Clint said, "but I think we should take a look in the kitchen, first."

"Damn it, Adams!"

"Where is it? This way?"

Clint started through the dining room, followed by the sheriff. Cantrell ran ahead of them stood in the way of the kitchen door.

"How'd you get that blood on your sleeve, Cantrell?" Clint asked.

"Wha—" The man looked down at his sleeve, and Clint pushed past him into the kitchen.

Mrs. Cantrell was sitting at the kitchen table—or rather, slumped over it. Her robe had fallen open, revealing her naked body. Her fair skin was covered with blood, which was dripping from the chair and pooling on the floor around her. There was a bloody knife on the kitchen table.

"Oh, boy," Glenister said.

Cantrell stood in the doorway, looking defeated.

"We may never be able to prove you poisoned those people, Cantrell," Clint said, "but this . . ." He looked at the sheriff. ". . . looks open-and-shut to me."

"You don't understand," Cantrell said. "She was wicked, evil. Look at her! She was horrible . . . and I couldn't . . . couldn't resist her!"

"Seems like you had control of everything in your life," Clint said, "except for your wife."

"Exactly," Cantrell said, "why I had to kill her."

Clint raised his eyebrows and looked at Sheriff Glenister, who nodded and took out his wrist irons.

Watch for

THE DEADLY CHEST

353rd novel in the exciting GUNSMITH series
from Jove

Coming in May!

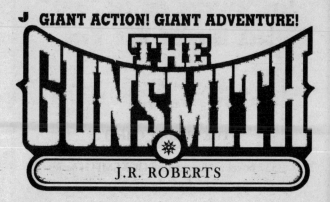

J **GIANT ACTION! GIANT ADVENTURE!**

THE GUNSMITH

J.R. ROBERTS

Little Sureshot And
The Wild West Show
(Gunsmith Giant #9)

Dead Weight
(Gunsmith Giant #10)

Red Mountain
(Gunsmith Giant #11)

The Knights of Misery
(Gunsmith Giant #12)

The Marshal from Paris
(Gunsmith Giant #13)

Lincoln's Revenge
(Gunsmith Giant #14)

Andersonville Vengeance
(Gunsmith Giant #15)

penguin.com/actionwesterns

M455AS0510

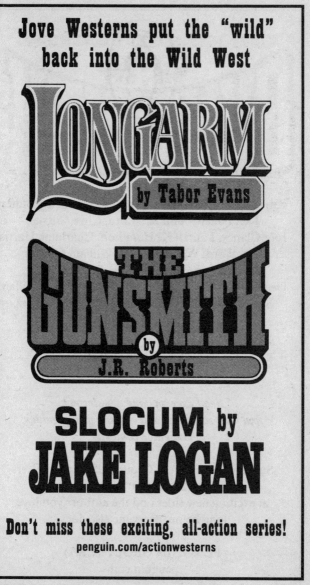

Penguin Group (USA) Online

What will you be reading tomorrow?

Patricia Cornwell, Nora Roberts, Catherine Coulter,
Ken Follett, John Sandford, Clive Cussler,
Tom Clancy, Laurell K. Hamilton, Charlaine Harris,
J. R. Ward, W.E.B. Griffin, William Gibson,
Robin Cook, Brian Jacques, Stephen King,
Dean Koontz, Eric Jerome Dickey, Terry McMillan,
Sue Monk Kidd, Amy Tan, Jayne Ann Krentz,
Daniel Silva, Kate Jacobs...

You'll find them all at
penguin.com

*Read excerpts and newsletters,
find tour schedules and reading group guides,
and enter contests.*

Subscribe to Penguin Group (USA) newsletters
and get an exclusive inside look
at exciting new titles and the authors you love
long before everyone else does.

PENGUIN GROUP (USA)
penguin.com